W9-CEW-514

ST. MARTIN'S

MINOTAUR

MYSTERIES

ST. MARTIN'S PAPERBACKS TITLES
BY IRENE ALLEN

QUAKER INDICTMENT
QUAKER TESTIMONY
QUAKER WITNESS

QUAKER WITNESS

IRENE ALLEN

St. Martin's Paperbacks

Published by arrangement with Villard Books, a division of Random House, Inc.

QUAKER WITNESS

Library of Congress Catalog Card Number: 93-262

ISBN: 0-312-97285-7

Printed in the United States of America

Villard Books hardcover edition / November 1993
St. Martin's Paperbacks edition / April 2001

St. Martin's Paperbacks are published by St. Martin's Press, 175 Fifth Avenue, New York, NY 10010.

10 9 8 7 6 5 4 3 2 1

FOR MY PARENTS

ACKNOWLEDGMENTS

The manuscript for this book was read and improved by my many friends whose generosity it is a pleasure to acknowledge:

Sarah Ruden, Anne Robinson, Eric Wegner, Betty Smith, Sharon Rogers, Clifford Harrison, Muriel Dresser, Walfred and Marianne Peterson.

Elizabeth Zbinden provided an important correction about the oxygen line described in the book, and Armand Larive gave me theological advice about repentance. My agent, Clyde Taylor, did his best to keep the manuscript on a firm footing.

This book is fiction. The characters within it are not meant to resemble actual people, living or dead, and Harvard's paleontology department is imaginary.

CHAPTER ONE

They shall run and not be weary.
ISAIAH 40:31

Lent began in Massachusetts with falling temperatures. Canadian winds brought record lows to New England on Ash Wednesday and February became crushingly cold. Near the shore in Boston, temperatures did not drop below zero, but in Cambridge it was 10 below on several nights. In the western suburbs, farther from the moderating effects of the ocean, the lows were even more bitter.

Two homeless men in Cambridge died of exposure the second night of the cold snap. The *Boston Globe* lamented the deaths in a long essay on its opinion page, a Bostonian ritual. As in winters past, the publicity surrounding the deaths prompted the police toward modest efforts to round up the homeless at night and take them to shelters.

By the third week of February, every soft or flexible thing in greater Boston had frozen as hard as granite. The rubber gaskets around the doors of the subway cars cracked and split as they hardened. Sea spray fell on the piers in Boston and froze into foot-thick crusts of feathery marble. The muddy waters of the Concord River were covered by a film, then a sheet, then a slab of dirty ice. The Charles River, separating Cambridge from Boston, turned solid a day later.

While the Charles's ice was still thin, some Harvard students went skating. In the middle of a sunny afternoon, a two-hundred-pound freshman broke through the ice where the current had undermined it. He was pulled out of the water alive by his friends. The university police stepped up efforts to keep reckless undergraduates off the river, but after forty-eight hours more of severe cold, the ice on the Charles was so thick that even heavy students could walk across the river safely.

One bitter but sunny afternoon late in February, a young woman ran coatless out of the main door of Harvard's paleontology building. Janet Stevens was a graduate student. Scientific research was her life. It was a life that she loved deeply, but as she ran away from her laboratory building she was sobbing, or sobbing as much as her rapid pace down Divinity Avenue and Oxford Street would allow. The cold air was so dry and biting that each of her ragged breaths hurt, but she gasped and ran onward, knowing that her only hope lay somewhere ahead.

She reached the end of Oxford Street and ducked into the Science Center. The sprawling, modern building was not her goal, but it allowed her to continue toward Harvard Yard while breathing warmer air and thawing her ears, hands, and feet. Now her tears, which had been in danger of freezing to her face, flowed freely. The warmth calmed her slightly, and she breathed more evenly. Janet turned down the hall that led to the Yard. As she rounded the corner, she saw Forrest Lang, a graduate student in her department, speaking with Professor Peter Kolakowski. She turned her face from them and hurried past. The professor, engrossed in the conversation, did not notice Janet. Forrest saw both her distress and her tears, and a look of disgust passed over his harsh features.

Despite her tears and her embarrassment at being seen in such a state, Janet could think clearly. She emerged from the southern door of the Science Center and ran the short distance through the cold across Harvard Yard to University Hall. For many who were at Harvard, or who had passed through it in their youth, the Yard stood at the center of the world. University Hall was a nineteenth-century, federalist-style building in the middle of the Yard. Gray and white, the building was surrounded by bare elms which gave the effect of a minor chord against the elegant stone. Just before reaching the statue of John Harvard, Janet ran up the steps and into the warmth of University Hall. The first door to which Janet came was the one which led to the Graduate School dean's office, the place that she was seeking.

The Graduate School office looked out onto the Yard in the direction of the science buildings and Oxford Street. Janet went in the open door. A neatly dressed woman at a desk looked up at her and said in a businesslike tone, "May I help you?"

Janet stopped for an instant, wondering how she could express what she wanted. She was no longer crying, but she was conscious that her face was tear-stained.

"Excuse me," she said. "I'm afraid I don't have an appointment, but I need to speak to the dean."

"The dean's life is ruled by his appointment book," answered the woman firmly. She added politely, "Is there anything I can help you with?"

Janet shook her head. "No. Maybe no one can help. But if anyone could, it would have to be a dean, I'm sure."

Janet felt her composure slipping, but her determination was based on desperation, and her desperation was deep. Gathering herself together, she looked up at the secretary and calmly said, "I'm sorry. Let me explain. I'm a graduate student here. My advisor is causing me such problems that I'm afraid to go into our lab anymore. I'm the only woman there, and terrible things happen when I'm alone with him. I can't go back. That's why I need to speak to the dean."

The woman nodded her graying head slowly. "What department are you in, and what's your advisor's name?"

"I'm in paleontology. His name is Paul Chadwick."

A look of pain passed across the face of the older woman. She motioned for Janet to sit down and said gently, "I'm not sure what can be done, but I'll speak to the dean when the person he's with has gone."

Janet sat and waited. Her limbs warmed up, and she realized how weary she was. It would be a challenge to get up from her chair when the time came, but the sufferings of her body seemed a minor problem compared to the unraveling of her professional life.

The secretary called someone on the phone and spoke in low tones. Janet listened idly but did not catch enough words to understand the conversation. She began to shiver, which was odd because she was now thoroughly warm. The shivering became more intense, running from her feet up her body. Janet was unconcerned by what she felt. Bizarre physical sensations seemed a minor cross to bear in her continuing education about academic life.

The phone call from Harvard Yard had gone to Byerly Hall in Radcliffe Yard. What the secretary said was sufficient to bring an assistant dean out into the bitter cold. Margaret North had not fully bundled up but simply jammed her lamb's wool hat on and strode out the door, still swinging her coat around her shoulders. It was not her custom to wear a hat; hats always squashed her mousse-set curls. But this winter's cold forced extreme measures even on deans. She buttoned her coat and wrapped a Black Watch plaid scarf around her neck, walking quickly toward University Hall. She sighed as she crossed Massachusetts Avenue. There was another crisis, she gathered, involving a young woman and an old man in a science department. If Dean North remembered correctly, this was her fifth such summons since taking her job one year ago.

She began unbuttoning and unwrapping as soon as she stepped into University Hall. She entered the outer office of the Graduate School of Arts and Sciences and nodded at the secretary. Neither woman spoke. It was obvious that the young woman seated near the window was the one who had occasioned the telephone summons. To the dean she appeared to be a typical student: she was young and slender, with long dark hair falling to her shoulders. Either the hair was naturally curly or the student regularly invested in permanents.

Crossing over with her coat, hat, and scarf on her arm, Margaret North introduced herself to Janet.

"I'm an assistant dean here," she began, her blue eyes searching the student's pale face, "and I'd be happy to speak to you until Dean Williams is free."

Janet looked up. She had stopped shivering and felt leaden. She looked at the older woman carefully, afraid she was being fobbed off on an underling. A woman dean, after all, would hardly be at the center of power at Harvard. But she knew her options were limited, so she nodded her head.

"OK," said the student. "Is there somewhere out of the way we could talk?"

At that moment one of the inner doors of the office opened, and an older man, wearing a tweed jacket and thick glasses, emerged.

"I'll see you tomorrow then, Bob," he said over his shoulder. Ignoring the three women gathered in the small outer office, he stepped out into the hallway and disappeared.

"Just a moment," said the secretary, rising rapidly and going into the inner office.

She returned a moment later with a smile. "You both can go in," she said and resumed her seat at the word processor nearest the outer door. As Janet slowly got up and stiffly moved toward the inner office, the phone rang. She heard the secretary saying, "I'm sorry, the dean is in a meeting now. May I take a message?"

Dean Robert Williams stood near a window of his office. He looked imposing against the bright sunlight. He motioned the women to have seats across from his desk. The dean wore a gray suit and dark tie; he was at least six foot two, with a head of thick gray hair. He looked like an important person and carried himself in keeping with that image. Janet had expected tweeds and corduroys. Perhaps, she reasoned with herself, high-level administrators had a dress code more appropriate to money raising in downtown Boston and New York than to the Ivy atmosphere of the Yard. In any event, she thought, this man might be able to help if he chose to listen.

Janet sat in her tiny dormitory room, looking at the dull screen of her word processor. Her unmade bed was only one foot away from the small desk on which the computer rested. She had had little sleep since talking with the deans, and dark circles rimmed her eyes. With a determined gesture, she opened the new document file but was unable to write anything on the empty screen. With a sigh, she stared out the window as vivid memories washed over her, memories that dated back to her first day of graduate school. Within minutes Janet began to shake again, just as she had while waiting in the dean's office. She felt nauseous and shuddered from head to toe. Quickly, she turned off the computer and dove onto her bed, crawling under the bedspread. A moment later, she pulled the bedclothes over her head. Only then did she feel some sense of security.

Two hours later Janet emerged from her cocoon and looked at her watch. She saw that she had missed lunch at the cafeteria. She went down to the first floor of the dormitory and bought a candy bar from a machine, quickly returning to her room. After eating half the bar, she felt satiated. Sitting down at the computer again, she began to write. After forty-five minutes of typing, she started to shake. Consuming the second half of the candy bar did not make the shuddering stop, and she turned off the computer and retreated once more to her bed.

The next two days passed in a similarly tortured fashion. Janet unplugged her phone, lost track of time, and was only dimly aware of how little she was eating. But slowly the document within the computer grew. She would reshape it and add more information to it with each sitting, then return to her bed to quiver under the covers. Although her confusion and pain were intense, she never considered quitting. She was on a one-way trip and knew she must go forward.

After three days of this, and one final long session of revisions, Janet was finished. She printed two copies of her letter for the deans and put them into the dormitory mail drop. Only then did she remember to make a backup of the file on a floppy disk, which read as follows:

Dear Dean Williams,

Last week you asked me to put my complaint against Professor Paul Chadwick in writing. I have done so, and in the process I have remembered much more than I was able to tell you in person. I'm a science student, not an English major, so this letter may not be well written. But every sentence is true and I would swear to everything I report here.

Paul Chadwick is an unusual person. No one on the faculty is more committed to excellent standards than he. He is able to see the important scientific variables in any situation. None of his publications is routine; they all have made a true contribution to my field. I chose to work with him because I wanted that sort of excellence in my own career. I did well in the courses I took from him, but I worked harder than I ever had as an undergraduate. He expects excellence from everybody and when he does not get it he flunks people out. Two of the men in my class dropped out because they got such low grades from him.

Unfortunately for me, Professor Chadwick is gifted at humiliating and intimidating women. His attacks are vicious. As you know, all graduate students in the sciences are dependent on their advisors not only for guidance on their research projects but also for money for their lab work and for their salaries. I have not been in a position to defend myself against his chronic attacks because I need both his advice and his funding.

To be specific about his behavior:

Professor Chadwick said to me when I first arrived here that women cannot do the quantitative work involved in science. He said that women need special (and lower) standards of admission to the department and special standards for class work because they can never acquire significant mathematical skills. He said that I had been admitted only because of affirmative action, and only affirmative action would get me my degree.

As a matter of fact, when I took classes from Professor Chadwick, I did all the problem sets on my own (most of the men worked together). I always got A's in my class work.

I hope that you or Dean North will check my qualifications for coming to Harvard and compare them to those the men had. Please compare the grades I earned to the grades of the men. (I know my grades are better; none of the men have a straight-A average. But I want you to check.) I am sure that Professor Chadwick's repeated statements about the lack of scientific ability of women in the department can be proven to be wrong.

Things got worse. Professor Chadwick wrote good evaluations of my work for the department records but when he spoke privately to me he told me I should drop out. When I first came to Harvard I thought he said such things because he was trying to get me to work harder. That was the best interpretation I could put on it. But now I can see that no matter how many A's a woman earns and no matter how many articles she publishes, she cannot be a "scientist" in the eyes of Paul Chadwick.

Beginning in my second year (after I had earned A's in his classes) Professor Chadwick started telling me "jokes" about prostitution and sex. He also would tell me how great he was in bed and how he would "wear his wife out." (I think they've been divorced for some time.) I said I did not want to hear about his life and I did not like his jokes, but he only laughed it off, saying I didn't have a sense of humor.

Sometime after he started telling me about his own sex life and telling me "jokes" about women he also began to use physical intimidation when I was alone with him in the lab or in his office. It was a common experience for me during that time that if I sat down in Professor Chadwick's office he would sit down next to me, putting his arm next to my arm. Before the conversation was over, his arm would be pressed up against mine. So, I learned to sit only in "Harvard chairs," the big chairs with fixed armrests, and I'd keep my arms inside the chair. This kept Professor

Chadwick several inches away from me.

Worse still was his coming into the lab when I was alone and standing face-to-face within a millimeter of me. This forced me to back up. A while after that, he started touching me. First he would put his arm around my shoulder. I would try to push him away, but I am much smaller than he is. He sometimes would come up behind me in lab and put his arm around my waist before I even knew he was in the room. When he took me by surprise like that it always made me cry. He would laugh.

From there, things got worse. This next part may be hard for you to believe, but it is true. Off and on this year Professor Chadwick has been seizing me whenever he sees me alone. He grabs my butt or my breasts. Then he usually pushes me away. I do not cry anymore, I just run from the room. I have talked to the men in my lab, but they have been no help. They tell me to ignore him. I tried to talk to the chairman of our department but he said I had a bad attitude, that I was exaggerating what had happened in the lab, and that I couldn't prove what I said.

I am still not sure why, but last week I just reached the limit of what I could take. I was alone in the lab and Professor Chadwick came in. He spoke foully, as usual, and then reached for me. He grabbed my lab coat which was unbuttoned. I slipped out of it (it's easy to get out of because all Harvard lab coats are made for men so they are much too big for me). I ran out of the building and I know I can never go back. I cannot endure one more day with that man.

And no other woman student should be allowed to
enter that laboratory!

Sincerely yours,
Janet Stevens

The day which had brought Janet Stevens outdoors
coatless was the coldest of February. After two weeks
of arctic conditions, temperatures became moderate
enough for snow to fall almost every day. Everything
in New England looked cleaner and brighter, and even
Cambridge lost its grimy appearance. People struggled to shovel the drifts and to stomp through the piles
of white fluff. Catholics could think of the shoveling
as Lenten penance, but others viewed the extra work
as simply a gift of life in the land settled by Puritans.

But God grants even Yankees a reprieve from winter. In early March the temperatures rose above freezing and stayed there day and night. The wind was
from the south. The gentle and moist air of New York
replaced Canadian winds. Small amounts of rain fell
every day or two, and the snows were rapidly beaten
back. Gutters filled with water and slush.

Janet Stevens's pain and trauma, witnessed by the
gates of Harvard Yard on the coldest day of the year,
did not ease as rapidly as the weather. After her jour-
ney to University Hall, she did not return to her department for two weeks. She spent most of that time
crying in her room. Further conversations with the
deans made it clear that the shame with which she
had been living since beginning graduate school was

going to become more, rather than less, intense. Restructuring a graduate student's life in mid-Ph.D. was not easy. Her research was dependent on the use of the equipment in her advisor's laboratory, and that equipment was controlled by him.

Janet felt unable to work at all, and for the first time in her life she was adrift. In the past, the rhythms of the intricate details of science had sustained her through whatever might be troubling her personal life, but now her intellectual life-support was absent just when she needed it most. As Janet was finding out, the process of filing a complaint against a professor for sexual harassment was long and demanding. The burden of proof was carried by the student, who had to publicly speak about things that might make a Marine sergeant shy, while her professor could assume an air of innocence quite credible to his colleagues.

Walking along the Charles on the first Monday of March, Janet was grateful for the warmer temperatures. She glanced idly at the ice breaking up on the river. She had spent the weekend quite paralyzed, wondering if she should declare herself crazy and go to the university infirmary, leave school entirely, or simply throw herself under the subway train in Harvard Square. This morning, however, the walk, the warm sun, and the movement of the river annealed some of her pain. She made a long tour of the Charles, walking downriver from Harvard to MIT and then back again. The walk seemed to strengthen her, and she put the subway tracks out of her mind.

Near the end of her walk, she thought about her

childhood, which had been easy and bright. She remembered Nancy, her best friend, with whom she had walked to and from grade school each day. They had played complex games of make-believe together during the summers; fantasies of lords and ladies and medieval towns. The games were always resolved when everything turned out right for all the characters. Nancy's older brother ridiculed their games as "girl stuff," but the two girls were easily and joyfully engrossed in their make-believe stories for long days on end. In the fourth grade, they had joined Camp Fire Girls, where both excelled at earning beads to decorate their Camp Fire Uniforms.

As she considered the wretched state of her present life, she found her feet taking her beyond the depressingly familiar streets of Harvard Square. She walked beyond Radcliffe and toward Longfellow Park. She knew that, as on the day she ran out of the paleontology building, she was moving on an irreversible path. There was a place, somewhere, that she had to reach. As Radcliffe sank from view, Janet realized that her feet were suggesting that she might be able to find what she needed at the Quaker Meetinghouse in Longfellow Park. Janet's parents had enrolled her in a Quaker school when she was young. Neither they nor she had been deeply religious, but Janet had retained from early childhood her warm memories of the Society of Friends. She had been attending Sunday morning Meeting in Cambridge on an occasional basis for quite some time. Because of the excruciating life she had been living at school, she deeply appreciated the silence and calm of Quaker worship. She had never said anything at Meeting nor introduced herself to anyone. That had been acceptable, both to the Friends and to her. Now, as Janet finished her walk, she instinctively turned away from the university and toward the Friends' Meetinghouse.

CHAPTER TWO

. . . they shall walk and not faint.
ISAIAH 40:31

On the first Monday of March, Elizabeth Elliot walked down Concord Avenue toward Longfellow Park. She was an older woman, a little stouter than ideal, with thick gray hair and an open face. It was her habit, late on Monday mornings, to go to the Quaker Meetinghouse and collect the mail as well as chat with Harriet Parker, the Meeting's secretary. Elizabeth was nearing the end of her first year as Clerk of Friends Meeting at Cambridge and found that the Clerkship filled the hours of her retirement quite fully. She enjoyed most of what the job entailed, and had no regrets about accepting the position. She was paid nothing, but the rewards of her labors were great.

Elizabeth sighed with pleasure as she walked. The 40-degree temperature and the strong sunlight were doing her good. Her nearly fruitless efforts to clear the snows of February from her sidewalk had given her shoulders and hands more arthritis pain than usual, but her joints felt a decade younger this morning. She took off her navy blue hat and held it in one hand, exposing her thinning gray hair to the sun. Her broad and open face was decorated with a half smile as she walked. Although she was unconscious of it, she almost always wore the beginnings of a smile. This accounted, in part, for why she was well liked by friends and neighbors.

Because of the warmth and the sun, the Clerk decided to walk through Mt. Auburn Cemetery before going to Meeting. The cemetery lay upriver from Longfellow Park, beyond Mt. Auburn Hospital. There were few green and open places left in Cambridge for walking, and residents had to take advantage of land set aside for other purposes. The inhabitants of the cemetery, presumably, did not mind casual visitors. Mt. Auburn was a favorite place for birders like Elizabeth, and walking among the dead was not distressing to her. When taking a walk or going on a birding trip, however, she avoided the section of the cemetery which held the remains of her husband, Michael. The grave was not a source of pain to the Clerk, but visiting it was always emotionally intense.

It had taken several years of widowhood for Elizabeth to think of herself as a single woman. She now occasionally went out with a widower in Meeting, a shy and quiet man named Neil Stevenson. He was good company, but, when Elizabeth thought of her life, she saw herself with her children and with Michael. She had, somehow, grown closer to Neil without feeling a true separation from her husband.

A passing cardinal arrested her attention, flaming
through the sky at the edge of Mt. Auburn. Looking
down, Elizabeth saw several juncos in the still barren
bushes. She walked into the cemetery and strolled
along its paths, hoping to see more birds. Two juncos
were her only reward within the grounds, although a
small flock of Canada geese passed, honking, over her
head on their way to the Charles. Things within the
cemetery still had a bleak, winter look, but Elizabeth
was glad she had come. Studying the trees, she could
detect the first signs of swelling buds. The sunlight
and shadows among the stones and on the pavement
were a delight. For the first time that year, the snowy
days of winter faded from her mind. She paused for
a rest and found herself reading one of the tomb-
stones.

WILLIAM RICHARD HUNTINGDON
BELOVED SON OF JOHN AND SARAH HUNTINGDON
BORN MAY 12, 1876
DIED DECEMBER 8, 1888

The marker was made of that familiar black-and-white
speckled rock, which Elizabeth's younger son, Andrew, an amateur geologist, had told her was granite.
Although the date on the stone was from the previous
century, the lettering was still easily read. She remembered the lectures about rocks that Andrew used to
give her on his vacations from college. He had
pointed out, in the tiny cemetery in Harvard Square,
that the slate grave markers of the seventeenth century

had not proven durable. The lettering on those handsome gray stones was almost completely worn away. Granite, Elizabeth remembered, had Andrew's recommendation for durability through the ages. But when the time had come to choose a stone for her husband, with space on it for herself as well, she had chosen marble. She liked the almost translucent stone's more gentle appearance.

As Elizabeth rested, she leaned against William Huntingdon's grave marker. She wondered if announcing one's life down through time was compatible with Quaker humility. A point could be made, she mused, to dispense with markers altogether. Perhaps she should have considered such things when Michael had died, but she had done the conventional thing in a moment of deep grief. And in the not distant future, she thought without fear, the same things will be done for me. God and I, after all, will soon be done with this body.

When she had read all the stones within sight, Elizabeth was rested. Standing up, she left the cemetery, crossed Mt. Auburn Street, and walked back downriver. The sun still shone brightly, but a few clouds were now visible in the west. She caught glimpses of the river as she walked, lined with cherry trees along its banks that would bloom within a month. Turning to the north, Elizabeth entered Longfellow Park. The only homeless person of her neighborhood whom she knew well, a man named Tim Schouweiler, sometimes lived in the park but had not been seen since the cold snap. Elizabeth was worried about him and looked hopefully around the benches near Mr. Longfellow's statue. But there was no one there.

The Clerk walked up the steps of the park, bringing Longfellow's grand old house into view, and then turned into the Meeting's property. Looking at her watch, she saw that it was almost noon. She entered the smaller building beside the Meetinghouse where the church office was located. The door was unlocked, so Harriet had not yet gone to lunch. Putting down her navy blue coat and hat on the bench just inside the door, Elizabeth walked into the secretary's office. Harriet was bent over her desk, struggling with the inner workings of a desktop calculator. She looked up as Elizabeth entered.

"Good morning, Friend," said Harriet. "I'm glad to see you. I've been wrestling with this off and on all morning and I can't get it to work. Do you understand these things?"

Elizabeth smiled and shook her head. "You young people are the only ones who can understand electronic gadgets." The Clerk had never touched a computer or a calculator, and her tone made it clear that she had no intention of beginning at the age of sixty-six.

The fifty-year-old Harriet laughed at the reference to her youth. "Your mail is here," she said, handing Elizabeth a pile of envelopes.

Elizabeth sat down and sorted through general junk mail, Quaker junk mail, and a few important items. She opened the letters which warranted her attention while Harriet packed the calculator away in a drawer,

talking to herself about the unreliability of such dev-
ilish instruments.

"Harriet," said the Clerk, looking up from a long,
hand-written epistle, "who is doing prison work for
the Meeting now?"

"Ralph Park is the main person," answered Harriet.
"Why?"

"This is a letter from a gentleman in Concord Cor-
rectional Facility who will be released soon. He says
he needs some Quaker visitation. He was apparently
part of the visitation ministry some Friends were doing at the prison a few years ago. What puzzles me
is that his name seems familiar. Do you remember a
John Anderson around here?"

"There are a lot of John Andersons in the world,
of course," answered Harriet. "But apart from the one
who ran for president as an independent, I can't place
any."

Elizabeth did not remember a John Anderson running for president, but she did not want to admit it.
"Is Ralph on Peace and Social Concerns?" she asked,
naming the committee within the Meeting which dealt
with social and political questions and should take an
interest in a prisoner's plea.

"He's Clerk of it! Your memory is slipping,
Friend."

"Indeed it is," answered Elizabeth unperturbed.
"I'll speak to him about this at Business Meeting."

"What's our main Business item for this month?"
asked Harriet.

"Your memory's slipping," said Elizabeth with a

smile. "It's the handicap-access question."

Harriet's temperament did not allow her to recognize irony. It was not that she disliked jokes at her expense, but humor of any sort was suspect to her. There was always tension in her relationship with the Clerk, who could speak facetiously on occasion.

"That's right, of course," said Harriet soberly. "I forgot."

Elizabeth sighed to herself. Some Quakers, good at heart as they were, could be a challenge. "Hugo Coleman on the Finance Committee hasn't forgot, I fear. He will have a lot to say," said Elizabeth. "Those long ramps cost quite a bit to build."

"Actually I think the bids he's got aren't so high. Because of the recession, maybe, contractors are working cheaply. But it will rather ruin the look of our fine building to have a concrete ramp running up to the front door," responded Harriet. She studied the Clerk's face for a clue to her opinion.

"Really?" said Elizabeth vaguely.

She was looking past Harriet through the office window at an unfamiliar young woman who was walking on the paving stones up to the front door of the Meetinghouse. The young person was moving slowly and looking down. She reminded Elizabeth of a picture of the children of Israel in captivity in Egypt. Elizabeth watched as the woman tried the door and found it locked.

"Look out the window, Friend," said the Clerk. "Do you know who that might be? I know her face from First-day Meetings, but I've never spoken to her, and I don't know her name."

"I don't know her, either," said Harriet promptly. "But she looks like a student. I'm afraid I can't keep track of all the students who come and go around here."

The young woman stood irresolutely at the Meetinghouse door, then tugged at it again.

"I'll see what I can do for her," said the Clerk and walked out the office and to the bigger building.

"Good morning," said Elizabeth as she crossed the alleyway. "May I help you?"

Janet Stevens could not bring herself to smile, although she recognized the gentle and friendly tones of an established Quaker at home at her Meeting.

"I'm sorry," she began in a strained voice. "I grew up in a little town in Pennsylvania where the Meetinghouse was always open. I just wanted to go inside for a while." She felt embarrassed and did not look Elizabeth in the eyes. Janet wanted to be alone in the worship room, but she did not want to use the word "prayer." Those two syllables seemed inappropriate from a science student, educated to secularism.

Elizabeth Elliot gathered that Janet was in need of whatever solace the Meetinghouse could bring. She introduced herself as she unlocked the doors and swung one of them open.

"We have to keep the doors locked, I'm afraid," explained the Clerk, "because of the troubles we've had with vandalism. It's very sad. I certainly envy Friends living in smaller towns who can do without locks. I've seen you around on First-days, haven't I? You're welcome to stay as long as you wish. I'll leave you alone; please lock up when you leave. You won't need a key." As she spoke, the two women moved indoors. Janet mumbled her name and said she was a student at Harvard. Elizabeth nodded her head and then clicked on the lights. She moved the thermostat up from its bottom-line setting to 70 degrees. "The Meeting has one of those new, small furnaces now," she explained, "so there will be some heat quite soon. Of course it takes a while to make much difference in this big room, so I recommend sitting by the radiator there in the corner."

Janet felt disoriented. Never since arriving at Harvard had she been treated respectfully, much less gently. Janet realized that Elizabeth was trusting her with the building and the furnace simply because she had attended some Meetings. She was not personally known to anyone here, yet she was being treated as a Friend. Tears quickly filled her eyes. She tried to speak but found her voice was blocked by emotion.

Seeing these signs of distress, Elizabeth was unsure whether she should leave, as had been her intention, or try to be more directly helpful. She motioned for Janet to sit down, then seated herself on the same bench but several feet away.

"I'm sorry," said Janet and then began to sob in deep gasps. She cried as violently and deeply as the day she had run down Oxford Street in the cold.

"Don't be sorry about coming here, if the Meeting-house is any help," Elizabeth said. The Clerk was unsure what more she might say. It would help, she thought, if she knew whether she were dealing with a fellow Quaker.

"Are you a Friend?" asked Elizabeth, regretting that her question might seem both abrupt and parochial.

Janet was not offended. Still sobbing she shook her head and said, "Not really."

Elizabeth waited quietly as the sobbing slowed.

"I went to a Friends' school when I was little," Janet began. "Because I was enrolled there, my parents went to the Meetinghouse at Christmas and Easter, but they're not Quakers. Vague Protestants, that's all."

A few sobs and some nose blowing stopped the speaker for a minute. Elizabeth remarked that her two boys had also attended Friends' schools. "Your phrase, 'vague Protestants,' might describe my oldest boy, too. Despite the fact that his mother is Clerk of this Meeting, it's been years since he's darkened the doorway here. My other son has become an Episcopalian. I'm not sure if that means he's a Protestant or not, come to think of it. Sorry to run on, I just meant to say I know that not all children in Quaker schools end up as members of the Society."

The student stopped sobbing. "When I was ten or so I was old enough to go to the Meetinghouse by myself. And I did, because my best friend from school always went. I have two years of First-day School and several dozen Meetings for Worship to my credit. And then here in Cambridge I've come off and on to your

Sunday Meetings. Really, I just come for the silence you Quakers are so good about. I leave as soon as Meeting is over; I've never introduced myself to anyone." She paused and then said more stiffly, "It's very kind to let me stay here, and I promise I won't disturb anything."

Looking around at the barren walls and simple benches that were the only objects in the room, Elizabeth smiled slightly. "I'm sure there is nothing you can disturb. I'm only sorry it will take a while for the heat to take hold." Elizabeth still had misgivings about leaving, but she respected the need to be alone. She rose to her feet. "I'll leave you now and go back to what I was doing across the walkway." Janet nodded her head but did not look up. "May God be with us all," murmured the Clerk as she quietly departed.

Elizabeth returned to the smaller building. The telephone rang in Harriet's office, and the secretary turned the call over to Elizabeth. It was a man in a Meeting in New York, asking how he could get a copy of the recorded minutes of New England Yearly Meeting from ten years ago. Elizabeth said he should call the Yearly Meeting office in western Massachusetts, but the New York Friend explained he had made his request there several times without positive result. The Clerk promised to inquire into the matter on the Friend's behalf and get back to him. Elizabeth collected her remaining mail and put on her coat. Harriet was locking up to go out to Harvard Square for lunch. As Elizabeth walked back outside she had a strong feeling that she and Harriet should not both leave, abandoning a distressed student in a cold and empty building. She said good-bye to Harriet and went back into the Meetinghouse.

The Clerk crossed the worship room to Janet, who was seated near the radiator. Elizabeth smiled apologetically and said, "I'll gladly leave, of course, but I just wanted to say that if there's anything you think I could do, I'd be glad to try."

Janet struggled to smile but started to cry again. "I'm sorry," she said, "there's nothing anybody can do. I'm too ashamed to speak about it."

Elizabeth sat down. Knowing that shame could lead people to complete silence, but that people who said they were too ashamed to talk probably wanted to, she waited a moment and then hazarded, "Is something wrong at school?"

"Yes," said Janet, nodding her head violently. "Yes, and it's been terribly wrong from the start. And the worst of it is, I feel it's all my fault." Tears threatened to interrupt the speaker again, but she held them in check. "My advisor is very important in my field. He's the biggest name around, even at Harvard. There aren't so many women in my field in the first place, and fewer than normal at Harvard. I've been the only woman in all the paleontology labs since I came here, and that's not a great situation."

"I'm sure," said Elizabeth, thinking for a moment about how protected her own life had been. "I'm sorry to confess my ignorance, but what exactly is paleontology?"

Janet was startled, but recovered. "It's the study of ancient life. People usually think of dinosaurs and fossil bones but what I do is chemistry. I study the chemistry of microscopic organisms as a clue to the way they evolved. My Ph.D. means several years of intensive lab work to gather new data that answers a scientific puzzle."

"Thank you," said the Quaker, "and forgive the interruption if you can. You were telling me about your laboratory."

"My advisor is the problem. His name is Paul Chadwick. I came here especially to work with him because he is the best in our field. He has an international reputation and it's based on fine work in several different areas. Some people are just in the right place at the right time—professionally, I mean—but he created several important theories, and most of his students have done important work. He has tough standards—for himself and for everyone. If your work passes muster with him, you know it's good. And he's taught me a lot. Strict lab procedure, careful data interpretation, and good critical thinking. Science is important to me, and Paul Chadwick does it awfully well. But in personal terms, it's all been terrible.

"He's impossible. Just impossible. I've never done anything to make him think the way he behaves is what I want." Again Janet paused for sobs, but then resumed. Slowly, with many detours for tears, she told Elizabeth her story. The older Quaker listened so quietly and deeply that Janet was able to tell of all her experiences, including many things she had felt unable to say to the deans. Elizabeth, as she listened, remembered Professor Anita Hill testifying before Congress about the fitness of a judge for the Supreme Court. She remembered her confusion listening to the testimony on television. This time, with a live person before her, she was not confused, only indignant on the woman's behalf. When Janet had finished explaining her situation she paused, her head dropping with exhaustion.

"I'm glad you've got away from that man," said the Clerk soberly. "That's the most important thing."

"It feels like it was all my fault!" cried Janet. "I know it's irrational to feel the way I do, but it's really hard to change once shame gets hold of you. I guess it makes some sense in terms of basic biology. Evolution has programmed us to think that all pain is our own fault, that we need to do something different to get away from it. It really feels like I've been doing something evil."

"But you haven't!" said Elizabeth firmly. "If you feel ashamed, then you're not the one who was causing the problem. That's the way the world works, I don't know why. Remember who was harming whom, here."

"That's right, I guess. It's good of you to look at it that way."

"No, it's not a matter of goodness. It's just the truth."

"No matter what Phyllis Schlafley says?" asked Janet with a bit of a smile.

"Absolutely not!" answered the Clerk seriously. "What can you do at school about this? Is there someone in charge of your department you can talk to?"

"Yes and no," answered Janet. She explained that she had gone to the dean of the Graduate School and met with him and an assistant dean. They had encouraged her to write a formal complaint. If she put it in writing, the deans told her, they could take action against Professor Chadwick.

"So I wrote down a lot of this stuff," said Janet. "It was the hardest thing I've ever done. The writing made me feel so hopeless."

The student began to weep again. Elizabeth prayed briefly that she might do and say the right thing.

Janet looked up and, for the first time, looked the Clerk in the face.

"It took me days and days to write. It's only three pages long, but the sentences came slowly. I worked hard at it because I wanted the complaint to be precise and one hundred percent the truth."

"Have you given what you wrote to the deans?"

"Yes, and they've started their investigation. Professor Chadwick has hired a lawyer to defend himself. All the men students in my field are writing him letters of support, because he asked them to. And what choice do they have? They want to get their degrees."

"They have as much choice as you or I," answered Elizabeth firmly.

"It's worse now than it ever was. I can't go back

to the lab because the other students—all those guys—don't want to be seen around me. I've got a bad rep in the department now; I'm a troublemaker. And Chadwick is still there. Just the sound of his voice makes me physically sick. I'm more distressed, just seeing him, than I used to be when I was working with him! I can't go back!"

Here Janet returned to sobs as deep as those which had begun the conversation. Elizabeth loosened her coat because of the increasing warmth in the room, and found she had Kleenex in her skirt pocket. She handed them to Janet. The young woman accepted the tissues and cried less violently.

"You don't have to go back," said Elizabeth. "Not ever! That's an important thing to keep in mind. You can go back when you want to, but nobody can make you return. For now, you need rest." The Clerk let the anger she felt come through her voice as she added, "If the deans don't respond to this situation soon, we'll hire a lawyer for you and sue." Elizabeth stopped, realizing that her empathy for Janet was carrying her into some thinking contrary to the spirit of Quakerism. She reverted to a more motherly attitude by saying, "Have you spoken about this to your parents? Your sisters or brothers?"

"I'm an only child. Normally I would talk to my parents—I mean I would have done so when I was a kid. But my mother is in the last stages of multiple sclerosis. She is confined to bed, and my father's life is organized around taking care of her. I can't burden them with my problems. My mother probably won't live to the fall."

"I'm so sorry," said the Clerk. "And you don't have many friends in your department, I'd guess, from whom you could get moral support."

"No. One guy is nice; the others aren't. And of course with no women students there, I've had no confidantes. As a college kid I had lots of friends, men and women, but none of them came to Boston when we graduated except me."

Looking at her watch, Elizabeth saw that it was after one o'clock. She inquired if Janet had eaten breakfast or lunch, a question which was answered with a shake of the head.

"I suppose I must be hungry," said the graduate student. "I've spent all morning, before coming here, I mean, walking along the Charles. I went down beyond MIT and then back up here."

"Would you be so kind as to come to my house for lunch?" asked Elizabeth. "I live on Concord Avenue, just four blocks from here. I have leftovers from Sunday's pot roast, so we can have some good sandwiches. And a can of soup seems called for, too." Elizabeth had always fed her sons alphabet soup when they were little and had to stay home sick from school. In this new and distressing situation, she fell back on what had worked for her as a mother.

"You're very kind, but I don't want to trouble you."

"No trouble. Quite the contrary! And you need food and rest before you can face this situation again."

Janet, realizing she was exhausted and grateful for the Quaker's concern, accepted the invitation. She would not have been able to accept help from any stranger, but this woman triggered her memories of elementary school and First-day lessons. And even if she did not know the Friends of Longfellow Park very well, she felt safe with Elizabeth.

After turning off the furnace and the lights, Elizabeth locked up and the two women left the Meeting-house. A serious wind was blowing away the sun and warmth of the morning. The Clerk and Janet walked toward Concord Avenue, the younger woman still looking at the ground. As Elizabeth steered Janet through the Episcopal Divinity School across Brattle Street from Longfellow Park, she caught a glimpse of one of the Harvard professors who was a member of Meeting. Elizabeth recognized Joel Timmermann by his stride, the gait of a self-assured man, and she was glad to see him. Although never active in Meeting life beyond attendance at worship on Sunday, he was a lifelong Quaker. He spoke often in Meeting for Worship and his messages were almost universally respected. Professor Timmermann was fifty and in the middle of a first-rate academic career. Undergraduate work at Yale had led to a Rhodes scholarship at Oxford followed by a return to Yale for a Ph.D. He had taken a teaching post at Harvard and, unlike virtually all of his colleagues in the same situation, he had been granted tenure. His writings, before and after the tenure decision, had redefined his field: the English revolutions of the seventeenth century. He was ex-

traordinarily productive, publishing a book on Crom-
well or the Stuarts every third year and several articles
on more varied topics in between. Professor Timmermann did not brag around Meeting, but he referred to
his success in subtle ways, and other Friends connected with the university spoke quietly about his academic exploits. He maintained a distance between
himself and the committees that did the work of
Quaker life. The committees took up a great deal of
their members' time and energy and that apparently
would have conflicted with his professional life. But
he was regular in his attendance on First-days and
respected for his vocal ministry on themes of personal
responsibility and the need for a more just society.

Elizabeth waved and beckoned to him as he crossed
the tiny street on the northern border of the Episcopalians' property. He nodded as the two women drew
near. Elizabeth wanted to ask for his advice about
Janet's situation and what might be done within the
university. A suggestion from a well-known and respected professor about what reasonably might be
done, with or without the deans, would be useful. The
adversarial approach of lawyers and written complaints was what deans understood, but Elizabeth
could see that Janet could not study in such a hostile
environment. But the Clerk saw no need for Janet to
be involved in the conversation for which she hoped.
So she simply smiled at Joel and said, "Would you
call me this evening, Friend?"

Joel Timmermann nodded. He went on his way,
apparently toward his home on Buckingham Street,

and the two women walked to Concord Avenue.

Janet was looking quite pale when Elizabeth seated her at the kitchen table. Putting on hot water, she searched her cupboards but found no alphabet soup. There was, however, a can of vegetable bean. After putting that on the stove, she made two thick sandwiches from cold beef roast. They were crumbly, but to Elizabeth they seemed full of nourishment.

Janet, in the meantime, had been looking out the window into Elizabeth's backyard. Despite the wind, several juncos and a number of sparrows were gathered at the bird feeder. Some of the seed had blown away, but the birds pecked at what remained. In Janet's present state of exhaustion, watching the birds counted as plenty of entertainment. She was still and quiet as Elizabeth fixed her lunch.

The two women ate, with the older of the pair supplying conversation about the birds in Cambridge and how altered the city was from what it had been in her youth. The Quaker was rewarded by the quantity of food that Janet put away. Everything set in front of the student disappeared. No doubt the lack of breakfast and a morning spent walking up and down the Charles explained this, but it was good to see the young woman still had enough basic health to eat. Elizabeth knew, from her own bouts with depression after her husband's death, that appetite could disappear entirely.

After eating, Elizabeth made a pot of tea. In the short time taken by the familiar task, Elizabeth saw that Janet began to nod.

"You are so kind to me," Janet said in a tone that made Elizabeth fear all the tears might come back. "I guess I'm awfully tired. I've really been on the edge the last few weeks."

"You're decompressing." Looking at Janet's pretty but pale face, Elizabeth asked, "Did you sleep well last night?"

"Hardly at all," was the mumbled reply.

"Why don't you lie down on the sofa while I clean up lunch? Then I could give you a lift back to where you live."

Janet knew that the least she could do for her hostess was help her clean up dishes, but she could not resist the thought of lying down. Perhaps it was the good food or the kindness of the Quaker. Something was making Janet relax and the result was a deep grogginess.

Janet lay down on the living room sofa and was asleep before Elizabeth had cleared lunch from the table. Seeing this, the Clerk opened the journal she kept under the salt and pepper on the counter. Like many Quakers, Elizabeth worked at keeping a journal, hoping that daily reflection and writing, like daily prayer, would keep her in touch with the spirit she sought in life. She made a long entry, recording all that Janet had told her and Elizabeth's thoughts about the general difficulties women can encounter in the male-dominated world of work. Elizabeth's mind traveled back to the Old Testament stories of Ruth and of Esther. They had struggled for respect as children of God in a world dominated by men. She wished she could recall the stories more clearly and she resolved to look them up when she next sat down with her Bible.

Janet awoke an hour after Elizabeth was done with her journal. She looked much better and her voice had some spirit. She was apologetic about having fallen asleep, thanked Elizabeth profusely for the lunch and for her sympathy, and said she needed to depart immediately. She lived in a dorm just north of the law school, only three or four blocks away, and she was adamant about declining a ride. Elizabeth extracted Janet's telephone number and address, then let her go on foot out into the windy day.

"I'll be in touch, Janet," the Quaker promised the student as she went out the door. "I'm sure more can be done than just have lawyers put everyone's back up. You need to feel safe at work even while the complaint is going forward. It's just a matter of explaining to the proper people what you're going through. The administrators should have thought of this themselves, it seems to me, but we can help them."

"I'm still not sure what you can do, Mrs. Elliot, but I very much appreciate your concern. I feel one hundred times better already."

"Don't lose faith. I'll be in touch," said the Quaker with her usual half smile.

Elizabeth spent the rest of the day baking a cherry pie and some quick bread. As suppertime approached she thought of her lifelong friend and fellow Quaker Patience Silverstone. Calling and finding her at home, the Clerk asked if she might come over for a talk.

"That would be wonderful," replied Patience. "I'm always glad to see thee, of course, and I need the help of a young person this evening to take the garbage can out to the curb."

Elizabeth was not offended at being thought useful and young. She put on her navy blue coat and matching hat and walked out into the late afternoon twilight. Fatigue from her long walk in the morning and the intense time spent with Janet was beginning to tell on her, but Patience lived just beyond the Meetinghouse, a mere seven blocks away from Concord Avenue, and the walk went quickly. She arrived before her nose got cold.

Elizabeth knew which side of Patience's house harbored the garbage can, and she carried it out to the curb, not without difficulty, before knocking at the front door. Patience let her in and greeted her old friend. The two women sat in the kitchen, the warmest room in the house, and Elizabeth was pleased to see that a teapot was in the center of the kitchen table.

"I made something hot for thee," said Patience and poured out Earl Grey for them both.

Elizabeth was glad that her friend was looking well. Although Patience was seventy-five years old, she had maintained both her physical and mental energy, throwing herself into the life of her neighborhood and Meeting. Her health had clearly benefited from her active life. She was now having trouble with hip and back pain, however, and this had led to a physical therapy regime. But she was still busy with Meeting work each day. Most of the work was done from her home, but she accomplished a great deal.

Patience's white hair complemented her gray-blue dress and matching shoes. Like Elizabeth, Patience had been raised in an era in which people still dressed as well as they reasonably could, even at home. For both of the women, First-days were for one's "Sunday best." This meant a dress and stockings, whatever the weather might be. But in keeping with Quaker simplicity, muted colors, conservative styles, and sensible shoes were the norm. Earrings and other fancy jewelry were frowned on by older Quakers as worldly and vain. Younger women upheld Quaker simplicity with brighter colors, African fabrics, and handmade jewelry, but Patience and Elizabeth still lived in keeping with earlier standards.

"Many thanks." The Clerk sighed, settling back in her chair with the cup and saucer in her hands. "I had an unusual encounter today, Friend, that I'd like to tell you about."

Elizabeth related all that Janet had told her, being careful to describe not just what the young woman had said, but her evident distress. Patience listened carefully and deeply, unafraid to hear. Empathy showed on her face as Elizabeth proceeded with the story. When the Clerk was done, the older woman slowly shook her head from side to side. Patience had never experienced harassment, but a lifetime of listening to people in Quaker service made it possible for her to empathize with victimization.

"The harm we do each other in this life can be great," she said softly when Elizabeth was done. "And at a university!"

"I hope there is something that Harvard can do to make her day-to-day life tolerable. She shouldn't be expected to make a written complaint one day, and then walk back into the same lab the next. Imagine the hostility of her professor!"

"And the other students and teachers have not been helpful?" asked Patience.

"They've not been responsive. It's unlikely they'll become so now."

"Change is always possible. God is at work through us, after all. But thee and I both know that it is difficult to understand we've been wrong. Especially— and this is strange—if we've been wrong in a way that caused daily suffering."

"Yes, but I would hope that the deans might understand that, rather than just focusing on their legalistic complaint process."

"Perhaps thee could speak to them on the student's behalf," said Patience.

"I'd be glad to do that, of course, if I have Janet's blessing for it. I expect to talk to Joel Timmermann this evening and see if he has any suggestions," said Elizabeth, rising from the table.

"Good," replied Patience. "And I will keep the young woman in my prayers."

The two women wished each other a good night and Elizabeth departed for home.

Elizabeth's supper that evening was a piece of left-over chicken and some of the new quick bread. She dispatched the meal quickly. When she was finished, the telephone rang. As she had hoped, it was Joel Timmermann on the line.

"What's on your mind?" he asked in a friendly tone.

Elizabeth explained how she had met Janet, described the state she had been in at the Meetinghouse, and related what she had said. Joel made no response as the long narrative unfolded, and Elizabeth was greeted with silence when she was done. Silence is not an unusual part of Quaker conversation, and the Clerk waited for the respected Friend to feel clear to speak.

Eventually he said, "These cases have always puzzled me, Elizabeth. Women seem able to take care of themselves in many situations, but sometimes not in an educational setting. If the professor does or says things the young woman doesn't appreciate, I'm sure all she need do is tell him so."

Elizabeth was unprepared for such a response. Exasperation flared up within her and she said, "She has told him to stop! What can a student do if a teacher refuses to hear!"

"I doubt that he is deaf," answered Joel with evident conviction. "She simply has misunderstood and hasn't made it clear to him how she feels. She should speak up. All this could be resolved."

"You aren't listening, Friend," responded the Clerk firmly. "I'm sure she has done all that a student, a young woman, can do to protect herself from misogynistic behavior. What he's been doing isn't for sex, it's to dominate her personally. And she's trapped in that program, trapped by her desire to get the education and the degree for which she enrolled. She's a right to those things, after all!"

"I don't have the particulars of the situation, of course," responded Joel in a distant and professorial manner, "but then neither do you. Remember, Friend, you have only heard one side of this story."

"I'll remember that. And much more than that," responded Elizabeth, feeling dizzy with distress. She said good night and hung up the telephone quickly.

"What willful blindness!" exclaimed Elizabeth to her cat, who lay curled up on one of the kitchen chairs. "Anyone who saw Janet could tell what had been happening! How can a Friend take such an attitude!"

Sparkle looked up at her mistress but did not answer. Elizabeth cleared away her supper things with a noisy clatter and did the dishes, still muttering to herself about cowardice and chauvinism. As she was rinsing the last suds down the sink the phone rang again.

The Clerk tried to take her anger out of her voice. "Hello," she said flatly.

"Oh, Mrs. Elliot, I'm sorry to disturb you again!" It was Janet's voice, clouded by sobs.

"It's just that I don't know what to do! The police

came to my dorm to question me. My advisor is dead. They found his body in the lab this morning. They think he was murdered. I was asked to come to the police station in Central Square by a Detective Burnham of the homicide department. They're asking all sorts of questions about me and my advisor. And about where I was yesterday and this morning."

Elizabeth thought quickly and said, "You're with Burnham now?"

"Yes," said Janet, still crying. "I'm not sure if I should answer his questions or not. I said I wanted to check with you and a lawyer."

"Don't say anything, Janet! An attorney should be with you if you are going to answer any questions. Tell the police that. Say that I'll be right down and I'll bring a lawyer."

CHAPTER THREE

But they that wait upon the Lord shall renew their
strength. . . .
ISAIAH 40:31

As soon as her conversation with Janet was over, Elizabeth telephoned Bill Hoffman, the only Quaker trained in law whom she knew. He had been a lawyer and was now a judge for the Commonwealth of Massachusetts. Bill was in his mid-forties and a lifelong Friend. He was not known in Quaker circles for much besides his family's money and the generous gifts to religious projects which it made possible. But Elizabeth thought she could rely on him in the present crisis. Unlike Bill, but like most Quakers, Elizabeth had a deep distrust of the legal system. The law, she thought, was based on violent enforcement of a code not always designed with the good of the community in mind. But to many it seemed a necessary evil, a better system than anarchy.

There was no answer at Bill's apartment, but knowing the work habits of judges, the Clerk called him at his office. Although he sounded surprised to hear from her, it was clear he was not displeased. She succinctly explained the situation and asked him how she could quickly produce a lawyer for Janet.

"The student needs a good criminal attorney," said the judicious Hoffman. "I can give you a phone number of one, an old friend of mine from school. If you can reach him, mention my name, and I'm sure he'll be glad to help."

Elizabeth took down the number and called Doug Gibson, Esquire. She explained that William Hoffman had given her his number, described the present crisis, and asked if he could help.

"Anything for Bill," said Doug cheerfully. "Tonight will be *pro bono*. If there's lots of work after that, I'll send the bill to the judge. He can count it as part of his religious work!"

Elizabeth was not sure if the lawyer was joking, but she agreed to meet Mr. Gibson in Central Square shortly. She hurried down Concord Avenue and across Cambridge Common to the subway. She arrived at the police station a few minutes later. A man at the door introduced himself as Doug Gibson. His good suit and close haircut met with Elizabeth's approval, and the two of them went inside. They went up a floor to Detective Burnham's office. When they arrived, the detective rose from his chair and gave Elizabeth a respectful greeting.

Detective Stewart Burnham was a biggish man, pushing fifty and neatly dressed. He wore a charcoal gray suit which Elizabeth could not help eyeing. It was well made and was new since Elizabeth had crossed paths with Burnham the previous fall. His tie was gray wool with thin maroon stripes and was set off by his immaculate and stiffly ironed white shirt. Elizabeth noted with a kind of satisfaction that the detective was one of the few left in his generation to wear 100 percent cotton shirts and have the laundry load them with starch. She had always starched her husband's white shirts heavily. She smiled at the detective. He looked uneasily at her, but did in the end give her a brief smile. He waved Gibson to a chair but invited the Quaker to wait in the hall.

"Only lawyers can be present for interrogations, Mrs. Elliot. But it's likely that Janet will be free to leave when we're done here, and you can wait down the hall in the lounge. I'll show you where."

Elizabeth was disappointed but followed the detective out into the hall and down toward a little cubicle only a policeman would call a lounge. She took the opportunity to say, "Mr. Burnham, I do hope you'll be gentle with that girl. She's been through terrible stress, lately."

"I never grill anyone, Mrs. Elliot. We policemen don't use rubber hoses. But I have a job to do, and I do it by the book. You stay here and, with luck, your young woman will be free to go when I'm done." Elizabeth sat down and Burnham went back, calling down the hallway in the opposite direction for Janet to be brought in.

The Quaker poked her head out into the hall and saw Janet, escorted by a police matron. The student looked small and frightened, but she smiled at Elizabeth before going into the detective's office.

The door to Burnham's office closed, and the matron went down the corridor and disappeared. Without hesitation, Elizabeth walked quietly down the hall and stood beside the detective's door. It had a glass panel in its upper half, and the Quaker was careful not to allow her shadow to fall on it. The hallway was filled with an evening hush; everyone with any choice in the matter had long ago gone home. The office door had an unusually high gap between it and the tile floor, and Elizabeth's sharp hearing could detect what was being said within.

"I have only routine questions for you, Miss Stevens," said Burnham. "As you have gathered, Professor Paul Chadwick has been murdered. He was found dead in his laboratory at Harvard this morning. A custodian found him, and a secretary called nine-one-one. We know Professor Chadwick was alive on Sunday morning because he was seen eating brunch in Harvard Square by one of his senior colleagues. That's been confirmed by the staff of the restaurant. But after that we know very little. Where were you from Sunday noon until nine A.M. today? Please take your time and answer carefully."

"I ate lunch yesterday at the student cafeteria in the law school, next to my dorm at Harvard. I ate with a man from my hall in the dorm named Bob Spellman. He's a Ph.D. student in geology. We were both pretty down, I guess, and we took a long time over lunch. He's been having trouble with his grades, and I've been having trouble with my advisor."

"Professor Chadwick," said Burnham's voice.

"I've had many personal problems with him. As you probably know, I've filed a harassment complaint against him." There was a pause and then Janet suddenly said, "I'm glad he's dead. I really am! I know that's a terrible thing to say, but he's tormented me for years. But I never thought of killing him, and I certainly never tried to do so."

The second half of Janet's statement was complicated for Elizabeth by the sound of Doug Gibson's voice telling her to be quiet.

"When did you and this Bob Spellman leave the cafeteria?" asked Burnham, apparently unperturbed by Janet's emotion or the lawyer's interruption.

"It was about one thirty, I'd say. I left Bob then, and he went back to the dorm. I went to the Square."

"Harvard Square?" asked Burnham.

"Yes, I went to Wordsworth and browsed there for a little while and then went to the Coop. I spent a lot of time in the history section in both bookstores."

"Your area is science, is it not?"

"Yes, but I like to read history. To relax," said Janet simply.

"Did you buy anything at either place?"

"No. Nothing much seems interesting to me anymore. I've been feeling awfully blue. James Allison has a new book out and I looked through it. But it seems to cover the same themes he's done before," said Janet. She added with a trace of confusion, "He writes on twelfth-century England."

"And then?" asked Burnham.

"I suppose it was about three. I went back to my dorm and spent the rest of the afternoon lying down in my room. Some people were having pizza in the lounge in the early evening. I had a slice. My next-door neighbor in the dorm, Maggy Billings, was there and she can vouch for me. But I only stayed for five minutes and then I went back to my room."

"Do you have a roommate?"

"No, all the rooms are singles. I guess no one can say where I was, really, for most of the day."

"Did you stay in your room all night?"

"Yes. I didn't sleep, because of feeling so terrible, but in the morning I got up early. About seven A.M. I walked a bit around Harvard, just to calm my mind. At that hour, it's a quiet place. I skipped breakfast and walked down the Charles to MIT and then back. Then I went through the square. I got to Friends Meeting sometime before noon."

On her side of the doorway, Elizabeth nodded to herself.

"Did you go into your department in the paleontology building in the morning?" asked Burnham.

"Yes. I hadn't been in for a long time because of the complaint and everything. My advisor's secretary, Ruth Markham, has been nice to me: she puts my mail in a Harvard envelope and sends it over to my dorm. But nothing had come for a week, so I thought maybe Ruth'd forgotten. She has lots of other stuff to do. Around half past seven, I think, I went into the first floor of the building, and got my mail from my box. There were two letters, so I was glad I'd gone in. But

I went right out again. I spent maybe one minute in the building and it was only on the first floor."

Elizabeth Elliot had been listening intently. By fortunate coincidence, Ruth Markham was a longtime member of Friends Meeting. Now that the Clerk thought about it, she remembered that Ruth was a secretary at Harvard, although Elizabeth had never known which department she worked in.

"Did you see anyone there?"

"No. And apart from just checking my box this morning, I haven't really been in to work since the third week of February, when I first went to the deans. The day that was so terribly cold and broke all the records, that was the last day I was in the labs."

There was a pause, and Elizabeth listened to a phone ring somewhere down the hallway.

"Have you ever used the apparatus called the 'oxygen line' in Professor Chadwick's lab?" asked the detective.

"Sure, I use the line," said Janet. "That's how I prepare my diatom and phytoplankton samples for the mass spec. They're marine animals, both microscopic organisms, that account for a lot of the sediments on the ocean floor. If the sediments get compacted, it becomes hard. Like rock. But before that stage it's soft, like mud, but the skeletons of the microorganisms are hard. The tiny animals are the stuff that's used in scouring powder, actually. I'm studying it because the microorganisms were crucial to the development of life on earth and we've got a good record of them in rocks going back to when the earth was young."

"Can you explain how the 'oxygen line' works? Why is it called that, anyway?" asked Burnham. "It looks like a spaghetti of glass tubes."

"It looks more complex than it is," she said. "All those tubes are interconnected, so there's really only one route through them. That's why it's a 'line.' The twists that make for the spaghetti effect allow you to isolate gasses. You freeze them in the tubes by putting liquid nitrogen around the U-shapes, you see. Like a bath, with the nitrogen held around the outside of the tube in little insulated containers. There are valves at every point in the line you can open and close. You move gasses through the line like that. Separated, I mean."

The two men within the office were not certain they understood the student's explanation. Elizabeth's attention had been distracted by the sound of a door at the end of the hall. No one, however, appeared and she stayed at her post.

"But it's not just oxygen? There's some poisonous gas involved in it, isn't that right?" asked Burnham's voice.

"What'd a lab be without poisons?" Janet sighed. Doug Gibson cleared his throat, but his distressed client was oblivious of such subtlety. "The product you want from the line is carbon dioxide, because that goes into the mass spectrometer. It's not a noxious gas at all. The bad part of the operation is the first step. You have to reduce the biological silica, which is sort of like quartz, with chlorine pentafluoride gas. You're taking the oxygen out of this quartzlike stuff; that's what reduction means. So you see, chlorine pentafluoride is amazingly powerful. Silica is pretty sturdy, right? It's not easy to reduce." The graduate student, unaware that her lawyer was confused, added simply, "That gas would kill you if you breathed it. It has to be fully contained in the first part of the line."

"Did Professor Chadwick ever do these sample preparations using the line?"

"No. Only young professors and graduate students do the nitty-gritty work like that. He wouldn't even understand all the valves."

On her side of the door Elizabeth realized that understanding what had led Chadwick to be in the laboratory could be helpful in resolving the puzzle of his death.

"What was the cause of death?" asked Doug Gibson.

"The autopsy isn't finished. But inhalation of a toxic and corrosive gas is what seems likely," answered Burnham.

"Janet," said the lawyer, "I recommend you not answer any more questions at this time. That's your right."

Doug added, apparently to the detective, "My client is not able to say anything more at present."

"That's fine," said Burnham quickly. "That really covers all I have in mind for now, anyway. Thank you for your cooperation, Miss Stevens. You're welcome to go home, but stay around campus where I can reach you. Don't leave Cambridge."

Elizabeth walked quickly down the hall to return to her cubicle.

CHAPTER FOUR

Therefore is judgment far from us, neither does justice overtake us: We wait for light, but behold obscurity; for brightness, but we walk in darkness.

ISAIAH 59:9

Dawn on Tuesday came slowly to Cambridge, wearily pushing back the darkness. Thick rain clouds entirely covered the sky, holding the night's temperatures into the early morning.

The faithful who came to the 7 A.M. celebration of the mass at St. Paul's were few. They kept on their winter coats because the building was not heated on weekdays. The coats were wet with rain. Lent was heavy in the air, and the priest's homily was as cheerless as the weather. He spoke on modern man's departure from the holy, dwelling on the crippling personal sins of middle-class Americans in particular. Echoing the words of Jesus, he asked his parishioners, "Do you want to be healed? Do you wish to be reconciled?" It was clear he did not have much hope for an affirmative answer. Only the Eucharist spoke of fruitful possibilities.

Elizabeth Elliot awoke that morning feeling stiff

and tired. Had she been part of a denomination which observed Lent, she would have been in a proper mood for a homily like the one being delivered at St. Paul's. Every joint in her body felt frozen. She lay in bed for a moment, testing her powers of movement and listening to the rain on the roof. She got out of bed carefully and slowly, searching her groggy mind for what activities of the previous day might explain her pains. Quickly she remembered her long walk to Mt. Auburn, and her mind leapt forward to Janet Stevens.

The previous evening, Doug Gibson had gone back to his office from the police station, but Elizabeth had escorted Janet to her dorm. Elizabeth had promised the student that she would come by the next day and, remembering that promise, the Quaker felt a return of her previous day's energy. It was clear to her that the situation was quite serious from a legal standpoint. But it was equally as obvious to her that Janet was no killer. Her behavior yesterday morning had not been that of a calculating criminal but rather a victim crushed by circumstance.

As Elizabeth limped to the bathroom and got her arthritis medicine, she thought about Janet's situation. She believed that Detective Burnham was not an unjust man. But she knew that from his perspective, Janet was an obvious suspect. Janet might even be his leading suspect, given the animosity between her and her advisor.

After breakfast, and a double dose of the arthritis prescription, Elizabeth called Ruth Markham, hoping to reach her before she went to work. Ruth could be

contentious and difficult. In general, members of
Friends Meeting at Cambridge kept some distance between themselves and Ruth. She was approaching
fifty and was not happy about it, nor had internal
peace ever played a large part in her life. Ruth's hair
was grayer than Elizabeth's, who was fifteen years her
senior, and Ruth's posture was already stooped. She
had a husband and one son, both of whom she viewed
as a burden even though she was fond of them. She
had been a secretary at Harvard for a long time and
was as resentful of the institution as she was of her
family.

Ruth was a lifelong Friend and had worked in the
Sunday school, more properly called the First-day
school, since her own child entered kindergarten. She
often said that her labors were not appreciated by the
Meeting. Quakers relied on her because she was re-
liable: she had been doing the same thing each week
on behalf of other people's children for as long as
most Friends could remember.

Elizabeth knew Ruth well, and although they were
not good friends, Elizabeth respected her contribution
to Meeting life. The Clerk knew that despite many
layers of resentment and dissatisfaction, Ruth Markham was a concerned and responsible soul. Elizabeth
Elliot trusted her judgment of the men in her department at Harvard and felt comfortable in being guided
by Ruth's views of what had been happening there to
Janet.

"Good morning, Friend. I'm sorry to call you so
early but I needed to talk."

"It's OK," answered Ruth in a strained voice. "I was up."

"It may seem odd, but I'm concerned about some things that have been happening in your department at Harvard. Harassment and sudden death."

"Really? You know about all that? Well I don't mind telling you I feel at my wit's end. My job is the pits on a normal day, and now it's getting insane! The police were in my office all day yesterday because one of our professors died. Been killed, it seems. How did you know about that?"

"It's a long story; I'll get to it in a minute. What actually happened yesterday?"

"The professor was found by the custodian, who then came and got me. I looked to see who it was before calling nine-one-one. I guess it's murder. The police think so. To tell you the truth, I'm afraid to go to work today."

"That's understandable," replied Elizabeth gently. "I've seen people die—my mother and Michael, too—but I've never discovered a corpse. It would be so unexpected, I can see it'd be frightening."

"Exactly. I just don't know what I might find today."

"I gather you know a graduate student named Janet Stevens," said the Clerk, a note of question in her voice.

"Sure!" said Ruth. "She's a tough kid. I've known her since she enrolled. Why do you ask?"

"She's been coming to Meeting for a while now. Did you know that?"

"No! I've never seen her."

"She comes to the eleven o'clock worship. I often have care of that Meeting, and I've seen her, but I only learned her name yesterday."

"I have to go to the nine o'clock Meeting, of course, because I teach First-day school during the big Meeting at eleven. You miss a lot if you're in the First-day school program!"

"Janet came to the Meetinghouse yesterday," said Elizabeth, ignoring Ruth's self-pity. "She was absolutely worn out and discouraged. She and I ended up having a long talk. She told me she had made a written complaint against her advisor."

"Yes," answered Ruth, "like I said, she has guts. Paul Chadwick was a terrible man when it came to young women. He'd been a problem for a couple of decades, but with our all-male faculty, nothing had ever been done. I know all about Janet's complaint from the grapevine. I'm sure she's telling the truth, but whether she can prove it is another question. Come to think of it, with Chadwick dead, I guess she doesn't have to prove anything."

"I'm afraid she might have to prove her innocence. Of murder, that is. She was taken in for questioning by the homicide department last night. I went down to Central Square, with a lawyer recommended by our own Judge Hoffman, and tried to help her with the police interrogation. She was in terrible shape earlier in the day, and being hauled in by the police didn't help, of course."

"But she's a good kid! Surely even a policeman

can see that! Do they really suspect her of murder?"

"I think so. She had motive to kill him, by their standards, since there was plenty of animosity between them. And she had the means, it appears. They think he was killed by a poisonous gas in the lab, and Janet knew all about the apparatus that contains it."

"Just because she made a complaint against him, a complaint he richly deserved, doesn't mean she killed him! I'd have killed the lot of them several times over if it worked that way!"

"As your sister in Christ," answered Elizabeth half seriously, "I should remind you that Jesus tells us that our thoughts and desires are just as sinful as any actions based on them."

"Jesus was living in a world different from mine, Friend," replied Ruth briskly. "Anyway, I'm sorry Janet's suspected."

"There must be something we can do. Are you going in to work now, do you think? Could we meet for lunch?"

"Yes, I've got to go to work. I don't want to, but maybe it won't be as bad as yesterday. I think the cops are basically done in the lab, but I'll see what the gossips around the department are saying. Let's meet at twelve at the Greenhouse Café in the Square."

Elizabeth agreed, and wished Ruth well in her morning's work. After hanging up, the Clerk called Patience Silverstone, who answered on the second ring.

"I'm glad thee called," said the older Friend before Elizabeth could explain the previous evening's developments. "I've been thinking about that poor student. And praying, of course. There must be something to be done. Was Joel Timmermann helpful?"

"I wish I could say so! I don't understand that man at all. I explained the situation, just as Janet had done. The good Professor Timmermann seems to think that women students are responsible for any trouble they encounter with their teachers."

"Do tell me what he said," responded Patience gently.

Elizabeth related her conversation with Joel as nearly word for word as her memory allowed. She could not keep all the disappointment out of her voice as she finished.

"I assumed a Friend would do better than that," the Clerk concluded.

"I'm sorry that wisdom and sensitivity are not guaranteed Quaker qualities," said Patience with gentle amusement.

"If his attitude is typical of the men at Harvard— and from what Janet says, it is—it's no wonder she feels so crushed. I don't think it was really Professor Chadwick who harmed her so deeply. It was the lack of a decent response from those around her. She says that only the deans have taken a different attitude."

"We can thank the Lord that the deans, at least, are listening."

"I didn't try to correct Joel's thoughts. I must admit I was a little angry," said Elizabeth regretfully.

"The anger remains with thee," responded Patience. "But perhaps I can speak with Joel. We're not close, but we've known each other for many years. It's been quite a while since I engaged in any serious eldering."

Elizabeth smiled to herself. Patience was referring to the informal but powerful Quaker practice by which older and wiser Friends tried to shape the behavior of younger or thoughtless members of the Society. With a start the Clerk sat up straight and said, "You must have asked me about Joel at the beginning of this call. That got me started on my holier-than-thou feelings, and I forgot to tell you some terribly important news. Brace yourself, Friend. Professor Chadwick has been found dead in his lab at Harvard."

Elizabeth then related the information she had gathered from Detective Burnham and from Ruth. She described the interview in the police station, omitting only to tell the honest old Quaker that she had listened at the door.

"I'm extremely sorry to hear such sad, sad, news," said Patience. There was silence on the line as the older woman examined her thoughts. "I'm glad that William has been helpful in getting the right kind of lawyer. But that poor student must be suffering."

"Yes," said the Clerk. "I'm going over to her room this morning just to check up on her. In fact, I'd better go now, Patience. I'll call you again, if I may, and tell you how things develop. Meanwhile Janet and I could both use your prayers."

"And Joel Timmermann, as well," replied Patience.

*   *   *

Elizabeth arrived at Janet Stevens's dormitory shortly after 10 A.M. The rain had stopped and a brisk March wind was blowing the night's cold storm out to sea. The front doors of the dormitory were locked. But when two young men emerged from them, Elizabeth asked to be let inside, and one of them held the door open for her.

There were both men and women in the hallway that led to Janet's room. As always, Elizabeth felt uncomfortable about that. But she knew that many things were coed that in her youth had been strictly segregated. Times change, she reminded herself, and this system seemed to work.

As she walked to Janet's door, Elizabeth reflected that a young woman who had lived in a coed dorm for several years must know how to take care of herself. Whatever Joel Timmermann might say, it was clear to Elizabeth that his attitude toward the harassment problem was absurd. Worse, it was destructive. It was difficult to believe that a blame-the-victim mentality was found even in the Religious Society of Friends. Anger flashed once more through the Clerk, but was gone quickly. A half smile was on Elizabeth's face as she knocked on the student's door. Janet opened the door and waved Elizabeth into the tiny dorm room.

"I've come to see how you are," said Elizabeth simply and quietly. "Did you get some rest last night?"

"More than I expected," said Janet, who nonetheless had dark circles under her eyes. "I'm all confused. It's difficult to believe the man is dead."

Janet closed the door behind Elizabeth.

"Please sit down at the desk, Mrs. Elliot. I like to sit on the bed, anyway."

Elizabeth took the offered seat, the only chair in the room, and Janet perched on a corner of the bed.

"I've been thinking about this situation quite a bit," said the Quaker. "If it's a case of murder, then of course somebody must be a killer. I'm sure that's difficult for you to imagine, but it has to be true. Apart from you, were there any other people who have had trouble with Professor Chadwick?"

"Not like me," answered Janet. She thought a moment and continued more slowly: "There's been a lot of nastiness in my field lately, and Chadwick and his counterpart at MIT have been in the center of it. The research group in paleontology at MIT was very close to publishing an important piece two years ago. They had a lot of data that demanded a reinterpretation of one of the big theories of punctuated equilibrium. That's a type of evolutionary theory. Anyway, just before they submitted it, Chadwick submitted a short paper, really just a modeling work, that anticipated a lot of their results. The boys at MIT felt he had stolen from their work. But all he had done was listen to a talk one of them had given here and figure things out on his own."

"If you take an idea from someone else, aren't you supposed to acknowledge that?" asked Elizabeth.

"Yes and no. If you borrow a lot of thinking from somebody, you've got to say so. But he wasn't using their data, and he didn't quote from their stuff. He saw a good idea and developed it into a model that could explain a lot, once the data to confirm it had come in. It wasn't wrong. But it's sort of a gray area, and he certainly wasn't generous toward them.

"The same sort of thing happened just before I came, or so I'm told. One of Professor Chadwick's students here, a guy who quit with a master's degree, left some good work behind him. Chadwick got a paper out of it. He did acknowledge the student. I know that, because I've seen the paper. But the student should have been a coauthor. At least that would be the normal thing. But he and Chadwick were on bad terms, and he dropped out of the field, so Chadwick just went ahead and wrote the thing up. And so he gets credit for the work."

"If people in your lab worked well with each other, though, couldn't Dr. Chadwick benefit more? Or even if he worked in a cooperative way with the MIT people? If he were on good terms with his students, whether they dropped out or not, it seems to me you all would be a lot more productive."

Janet sighed. "It looks that way to me, too. But don't say that to the men. They're real competitors. They think talk like that is slop."

"Tell me about the other people in your lab. Aside from your advisor."

"OK," replied Janet. She paused to pull a blanket around her shoulders. "There's Eric Townsend and Forrest Lang. They came here at the same time, one year before I did. They were both undergraduates at

Princeton. I guess they were good friends there; at least they always talked that way when I was new. But there's some trouble between them now."

"What are they like?" asked Elizabeth in her most encouraging tone.

"Eric is a nice guy. He always wears a Walkman, and we tease him that he's losing his hearing. He'll finish up next year for sure. He didn't publish his senior thesis from Princeton. Forrest did get an article out of his, and he never lets us forget it. But Eric has done well at Harvard. He's got two articles in print already. And he's not a cutthroat type, which is rare for somebody who's successful in my field. I like him. His wife has a good job, downtown Boston somewhere, and they live in a great apartment in Newton that they invited me to once. Definitely not a student slum!"

"How did he get along with Professor Chadwick?"

"OK. Eric did some really good work. They get along well enough. Or got along, I should say. They were both fanatic Red Sox fans—Eric and Chadwick—and they talked about baseball all year round."

"My two boys follow the Red Sox, too," said Elizabeth. "When they were teenagers I sort of resented it. Their father and the boys would talk of nothing else during the summer. It left me out of the conversation."

"I know that feeling!" replied Janet. "We eat lunch together in the lab, and all the guys talk about is the Bruins and the Red Sox. And some other team. But

Eric is no worse than the rest of them about sports, and he's a nice guy."

"Did you ever talk to him about your advisor's behavior?"

"Yes. He said I had to put up with it. He told me to ignore it and just do my work."

"It's not the kind of thing that could be ignored," said Elizabeth slowly shaking her head. "Tell me about the others, please."

"Forrest Lang is a real jerk. He's supercompetitive and thinks everybody is out to steal his data or his ideas. He locks up his lab notebooks at night! He'll hardly talk to me at all. He's always upset about tiny things. Just before Christmas he yelled at me because my bench is always a mess. That's true, but it doesn't affect his bench."

"What's a bench?" asked the elder woman. The sun had emerged from the dark clouds of the morning and, as she spoke, the room became brighter.

"Like a counter. The place where you work," answered the student with a touch of surprise in her voice. She clearly considered it an obvious term.

"Did Forrest get along with your advisor?"

"Yes, in a general way. They didn't like each other, I'm sure. Nobody likes Forrest Lang. Or liked Chadwick, for that matter. But they got along. Forrest is doing some interesting stuff. He'll get published soon."

"Did your other professors have trouble with Dr. Chadwick, do you think?"

"No, I don't think so. They respect him a lot. He's

a real big name in my field. The biggest, I guess. He doesn't publish routine stuff, only things that really make a difference, and the other professors know that. There's a young prof in our department named Peter Kolakowski who's maybe going to be even more important than Chadwick, but that will take a few years. He's been producing amazing amounts of data himself. He's got several big articles out right now, as sole author. He's a pretty nice guy and I've talked to him a lot. He's not trouble for women.

"There's a student named Louis in his lab. He's doing well. He just put together a paper with Peter. I know Louis well, actually. We were dating in the fall, before I got sick of the department and everybody connected with it. I think Louis has personal, not just intellectual, integrity, which is pretty rare in research science. He still has a crush on me, I guess, judging by the notes he's left in my mailbox since I went to the deans."

Janet paused and shuddered. She looked away from Elizabeth as the sun disappeared behind a passing cloud.

"I admit, I was avoiding Louis while I was writing up that complaint; it's just that everything about the department was making me sick to my stomach. I wouldn't have liked Mother Teresa if she worked in that building, do you see? And now what I'm feeling is anger. Because he's dead, I guess. I was sitting here before you came, recalling all the disgusting things he used to do to me and the things he used to say. I'd still like to kill him! I've never felt this way. I'm surprised, actually, that so much anger can fit inside of me."

Elizabeth smiled slightly and thought to look at the time. It was almost noon.

"The anger doesn't surprise me. It may be that you are free to feel more because the man is dead. Don't act on the anger and you'll be OK. But I've got to be going, I'm afraid, to meet someone in the Square. I'll call you tomorrow, just to say hello and see how you are. Don't let things get you down."

"I'll try," said Janet with a weak smile. Despite fatigue and anger, however, she seemed much more settled than she had yesterday at Friends Meeting. Elizabeth, with motherly acuity, noted that some color was returning to Janet's face.

Elizabeth found a seat at the Greenhouse Café and in a few minutes, Ruth arrived. The secretary was look-ing cross as she entered the café but changed her ex-pression when she saw the Clerk.

"It's good to see a Friend," Ruth began, sitting down. "What a morning!"

"Were the police at your office again?"

"Yes, for a bit," answered Ruth, surveying the menu. "After they left I talked to the graduate students and picked up some interesting perspectives."

The waitress came and departed with the women's orders.

"Where shall I begin?"

"Could you tell me a bit about the students? What they're like and what they're saying? Let me ask you about them one by one. I think I know their names from Janet. One man in her lab is Eric Townsend, isn't that right?"

"Yes," said Ruth, "a pleasant young man, liked well enough around the department. It can be a little hard to say hello to him because he wears one of those portable radios. But he's a fine guy. I gather that his work has gone well. He was something of a star for Chadwick."

"Did they get along, do you think?"

"There's always some tension between graduate students and their advisors, especially when they're finishing their degrees. But, in a general way, I don't think Eric had trouble with Chadwick.

"Eric is saying that he was in the lab all morning Sunday and in the early afternoon. Chadwick came in about noon and they said hello to each other, but that's about all. Chadwick was in his office when Eric left. He thinks that was about two P.M.

"Eric thinks he and Chadwick were the only ones on the second floor for any length of time."

"Who is housed on the second floor?" asked Elizabeth.

"My office is there, and Chadwick's office, our conference room, a large room that's a walk-in freezer, and another storage room, and Chadwick's lab. And a closet for the janitor's stuff. The lab has the spaces where the students work."

"And that's where the 'oxygen line' is?" asked

Elizabeth, despite herself feeling some pride in her knowledge of such technical matters.

"That's right, and some other things, too. I'm also the secretary for Peter Kolakowski, but he and his student Louis Lazier are up on the third floor. They have to come downstairs to give me work. Louis was in the lab all day on Sunday, he says, but he stayed up on the third floor and didn't see the second-floor gang at all."

"What about Forrest Lang? Do you like him?"

"No," said Ruth. "I certainly don't. He's uptight and flies off the handle at the slightest things. He has a Texas twang that's sharper than his mind. His accent is enough to drive any Yankee bonkers. But Chadwick told me just last week that the experiment Forrest just finished has a highly impressive finding. The boy will be published and may make quite a name for himself even while he's a student. At least that's what Chadwick seemed to think.

"Forrest says he pulled an all-nighter in the lab on Friday night. He went home Saturday at ten A.M. and didn't come back until Monday morning, a bit after the custodian and I had found the body."

"Why would he work in the lab all night?"

Ruth laughed. "Oh, that's normal for rising young stars in lab science. They do it to get more done, and because it makes the work seem important and exciting. At least that's what I think. Forrest says he was at home on Sunday, setting up his new Macintosh. He bought a powerful and expensive one through the university. I could see how Eric might afford that, because his wife's an MBA. But Forrest is just a single student with no wife to support him. I don't know where kids in school get so much money! It was different when I was in my twenties, I can tell you." The waitress arrived with a BLT for Elizabeth and the dieter's special plate for Ruth. After a brief silence for prayer, awkwardly observed by Ruth, the women began to eat.

"Would you say that Janet did anything, however unconsciously, to merit some of the trouble she had with her professor? I don't mean, did she deserve it, but just is she the sort of person that often has trouble where others don't?"

"Heaven's no! What happened to her is no fault of Janet's! Chadwick is just plain sick. He's never had a successful woman Ph.D. student. Not in the years I've been there, anyway. They—the women, I mean—get weary of the abuse and drop out. Janet has had the courage to object, which is the right thing to do. But it's hell to be a whistle-blower. I couldn't do it, I'm sure. You know, when I think about it, it's not surprising that she's been coming to Meeting. She has the right basic ingredients to be a fierce Quaker, a real witness if you know what I mean. But she's still young, and it's been awfully hard on her to make this complaint. I think she's been really depressed by everything. I've been trying to remember to send her mail over to her dorm so that she doesn't have to come in for it because just being in the building is hard for her."

"The death of her tormentor is changing all that,"

said the Clerk. "She's a lot perkier today than yesterday. But angry, too."

"Great! She sure has reason to be angry. And like I said, she's young. But I'm doubly glad if she gets enough energy together to come back to the lab. I'd hate to think that slime like Paul could keep her away from her work, even after he's gone."

Ruth paused long enough to cut some resistant lettuce into small bits. "It was a power thing, really, not sex, between her and Chadwick. As usual, the department denied there was any problem."

"Why?" asked Elizabeth simply.

"Partly because Chadwick was so famous, and partly because if they admitted what a sick and unprofessional man he was around women, they would have had to do something about it."

Elizabeth wondered if that might explain something of Joel Timmermann's attitude as well. She surrendered her plate to the waitress and asked for tea. Ruth ordered a cup of decaffeinated coffee.

The two women sat silently for a minute. For the first time since Ruth had come, Elizabeth was conscious of the noise and buzz of the café. She drifted off for a moment into a daydream about confronting Joel Timmermann, but then she recalled her thoughts to the world of paleontology.

"Has anything strange been going on in your department? I mean, have day-to-day things been upset in any way?"

"Let me think," answered Ruth. "We're way behind on our photocopy budget. That means somebody is copying things without charging it to their grant. That happens sometimes, but it's worse than normal. The oldest professor we have has come down with a case of mono, if you can imagine that. The students wonder who he's been kissing. Someone spilled coffee over a completely filled out set of student loan forms I had typed up for Eric. I left them on the center of my desk one night, and when I came in in the morning they were ruined. The janitor swore it wasn't him, but I don't see who else is likely to be drinking coffee in off-hours at my desk. Nicest of all, I almost quit last month when the gentle Professor Chadwick yelled at me for having disturbed everything on his desk. I'd never gone into his office, so I knew he was off his rocker."

"What did he say?"

"What he said can't be repeated to a good soul like you. But I told him to shut up and explained I'd never been in his office. Eventually, he believed me. Maybe the custodian or the security man had moved some of his papers, although I can't imagine why. But he didn't say anything recently."

Ruth looked at her watch with a sigh. "I have to be getting back, Friend. I've only got half an hour for lunch. Do you want to walk me back to work? It's not so miserable out as it was this morning, and you might meet some of these characters I've been telling you about. Also, it might help me if you were to come. I've not been in the lab since finding the body, you see."

"Certainly," said Elizabeth quickly. "I'd be glad to come."

CHAPTER FIVE

He giveth power to the faint; and to them that have no might he increases strength.

ISAIAH 40:29

Ruth and Elizabeth arrived at the paleontology building and went up to the second floor. Ruth hung up her coat in her office and told her friend to do the same.

"Let's go look. The sooner I face it, the better," said the secretary. The two women walked down to the end of the hall. As they walked, Elizabeth inquired into the source of the dull, throbbing noise that seemed to echo throughout the floor.

"Oh, I don't know," answered Ruth. "Science departments often have unpleasant sounds. And occasionally loud ones, when some student's samples blow up. Or whatever. And there can be weird smells, too. The chemistry department here always reeks of acid. I worked there for eleven months. It was eight or nine years ago and sometimes I think I can still smell that acid tang in my clothes."

"Being a scientist must be a special calling," murmured Elizabeth.

The women reached the end of the hall. The secretary opened a door on which a sign said: CAUTION: CORROSIVE GASES AND HIGH TEMPERATURE REACTIONS: AUTHORIZED PERSONS ONLY. Elizabeth was tense as she entered the laboratory after Ruth. She did not know that she might have taken comfort in the absence of radiation warning signs.

"This is Chadwick's lab," said Ruth, looking around the room. "I know what some of the things are and what they're called. I don't understand the details, of course." Elizabeth, too, looked around the large room. In front of her was a stand, about the length of Elizabeth's kitchen, covered with dials, valves, and convoluted glass tubing. This, thought the Clerk, might be the "line" that Detective Burnham had asked Janet about. On the wall to the Clerk's left a counter held an assortment of strange containers made of brick and metal. The wall on the right had a short and squat instrument with small hoses and a computerlike face. One hose was draining into an open bucket on the floor. Elizabeth crossed over to the bucket where a foul-smelling fluid was steadily dripping into the pail.

"That's called an ion chromatograph," said Ruth. "I don't know what it does."

"It looks like a mixture of high tech and slop bucket," said the elder woman. "What strange people scientists must be."

"You get used to them," said Ruth.

Elizabeth moved back to the center of the room. "Is this the line I've heard about?"

"Yes," answered Ruth. "It's the thing that holds the awful gas. These things on the counter," added Ruth, waving to the left, "are high-temperature ovens."

"Where did you find the body?"

Ruth winced slightly but answered, "Just about where you're standing, between the line and the ovens. He was on his back, his mouth wide open, his hands up by his throat. I know now that he was dead, but when I first saw him, he really looked like he was in agony."

"Did you touch him?" asked Elizabeth gently.

"Well, yes, I did." She looked away from Elizabeth. "I touched one of his hands. I was speaking to him, you see, trying to get him to respond. But his hand was cold, like stone. It wasn't like a hand at all. So I said to Carl—the janitor, you know—that he should stand outside the door here and not let anyone in. I said I'd call for an ambulance. I dialed nine-one-one. The police came, too."

"Who got here first?"

"The ambulance people. They came out and said he was dead and that they'd wait for the police to arrive."

A young man in a Red Sox sweatshirt pushed open the door and walked in. He looked at Elizabeth, clearly puzzled, removed a Walkman radio from his ears, and said hello to Ruth.

"This is Eric Townsend, one of Professor Chadwick's students," said the secretary. "And this is a good friend of mine, Eric. Elizabeth Elliot. She was kind enough to come here to help me get over the willies."

"Hi," said Eric cheerfully, nodding his head at Elizabeth. "It's a difficult time for everybody," he said, looking at Ruth.

"It must be distressing to everyone who knew Professor Chadwick," said Elizabeth evenly. "How will his death affect you students? As far as your degree, I mean?"

"It's not a problem for me. I'm near enough to finishing that I can clear out pretty much anytime. Someone else will have to sign my thesis, of course, but I've already talked to Professor Scott. He's the chairman. He's ready to sign himself," said Eric, setting down his notebooks on what Elizabeth took to be a "bench." "My main stuff has already been published, you see, and it's pretty well regarded. I wish Janet's work was in print."

Eric looked at Ruth and asked, "Do you have any news of her?"

"Indirectly, only. Elizabeth has been helping her in dealing with the police. They questioned her down in Central Square. They know about the complaint, you see," finished Ruth.

"You know Janet?" asked Eric, clearly puzzled.

"Just a bit," answered Elizabeth. "She certainly has been under a lot of stress here."

"Yes," replied the young man. "I've tried to be supportive, but she's really had it rough. Chadwick could be an ass."

Elizabeth wondered what sort of behavior might qualify in this young man's mind as unsupportive.

Elizabeth changed her tone and asked, "Just out of curiosity, could you tell us a little bit about this line. The police were asking Janet about it."

"That Burnham fellow asked me about it too," replied Eric easily. "I can tell you the basic principles pretty easily."

Eric stood in front of the long stand and waved to the far end of it.

"That's the output end down there where the carbon dioxide gas is collected. That's what we run through the mass spectrometer. Carbon dioxide is a common gas. It's the stuff that makes Coke and club soda fizz."

"So it's not harmful," said Elizabeth.

"Right. But this part of the line is where we have to make the CO_2. The sample is silica. That's silicon bound with oxygen. It's a biological product of a lot of marine organisms, like diatoms, and it's one of the things we study here."

Elizabeth nodded her head. Ruth moved closer to hear better.

"You put the solid sample of material in here," continued Eric, pointing to a small chamber at the extreme end of the apparatus. "This part is all metal and is lined with platinum, which won't react to anything no matter what. Next you use the vacuum pump to remove the air from around the sample. Then you use this tank," he said, pointing to a metal cylinder, "to add chlorine pentafluoride gas to the sample chamber.

This stuff is so reducing that it actually extracts the oxygen from the silica, which is a pretty neat trick."

"Pretty neat, but also dangerous?"

"It's only dangerous to the sample, if you do everything right. The chlorine pentafluoride never leaves the line, or it's not supposed to. You turn this valve off, and move the oxygen gas forward to this section. The next step is completely burning the oxygen with carbon to get CO_2. That you do with heat and these carbon rods. It goes pretty quickly. After that, you move the gas along the line to here." He indicated a large U-turn in the glass tubing. "You freeze it to make sure it's pure. Sometimes there's a little water vapor or something in it, you see, and that will have a different freezing point. That's the principle you use to separate gases from one another. Then you move it along the line to the end. We put it in these bigger glass tubes. That's the gas that goes into the mass spec." Eric turned to look at Elizabeth.

Elizabeth decided she need only be interested in the first section of the apparatus. She called Eric's attention back to it.

"If the carbon penta-whatever gas escapes from this end," she said, waving her hand at the metal cylinder, "exactly what happens?"

"It would reduce all the oxides it contacted. That means it would take the oxygen out of plastics and things like that. It would be diluted by all the air in this room, so it wouldn't reduce the window glass or the wood. But human tissue is delicate and reactive. You'd die if you breathed the air in here."

"See this film on the floor tiles?" he asked, calling Elizabeth's attention to a white frosty coating on the dark tiles. "That wasn't there before this weekend. It's the result of the carbon pentafluoride, reacting with the floor wax. Things could have been worse, though. This hood fan is always running," he said, waving a hand at a small section of counter that had a metal rooflike top to it. "It's pumping air out of here, up to a chimney on the roof. That's where the gas went. It was pumped out for all of Cambridge to deal with. But outside it's so diluted it probably wasn't worse around here than things usually are on a smoggy day.

"Anyway, I assume that's what happened. I know the police think so, too. At least they were asking me all sorts of questions about what gases we use and how long things stay in the air here when they're released."

"How long would the room have been dangerous?" asked Elizabeth.

"The hood fan empties this room every ninety minutes."

A loud clanking sound from the counter made Elizabeth and Ruth start. Eric smiled and said, "Don't worry. That's just one of the high-temperature ovens coming on. I've got it set on a timer."

"Do you have a guess how the police think the gas was released?" asked Elizabeth.

"When they called me in to look over things and explain them, there was a valve operated on a timer, just above the canister of chlorine pentafluoride. It wasn't there before, I assure you. The manual valves on the line were open. So when the timer went off, the canister emptied into the room. It would all have happened fast. Ten seconds and the room would have been full of the gas. The police took that timer and the canister away with them."

He walked across to the right-hand wall of the laboratory. "But I've got to do some routine maintenance on the ion chromatograph this afternoon. And then both Louis and I have analyses we need to run on it. So if you two ladies will excuse me?"

"Of course. Thank you for the explanations," answered Elizabeth. She looked at Ruth, and the women moved to the door as Eric put on his headphones. Just as she and Ruth entered the hallway, a young man shot out of the stairway, scowling.

"This is Forrest Lang, Elizabeth," said Ruth. The secretary frowned at the student as she added stiffly, "Elizabeth Elliot."

The young man nodded his head at Elizabeth, stepped around the two women, and entered the laboratory.

"He's a real outgoing sort," said Ruth.

"So I see," responded Elizabeth. "Is he always so social?"

"Basically. He's intense about his work. Neurotic, I think."

"Eric seems to think Forrest's work is going well," observed Elizabeth. "And that fits with what Professor Chadwick said to you."

"Which just means he'll become another tenured ass around here," said Ruth. "From Texas!"

Ruth entered her office ahead of Elizabeth. The elder woman asked, "Did Professor Chadwick have a family here in Cambridge?"

"No, he had no kids," answered the secretary. "His wife left him ten years ago, and he's lived alone since then."

"I'll be going," said Elizabeth quietly, taking her coat down from the hook behind the door. Although she knew her timing was not the best, as Clerk she could not help but add, "Will we see you at the Business Meeting tonight, Friend? We've got to address the handicap access question again. Resolving our differences about it requires everybody be present."

"I'll come if I can," replied Ruth.

Knowing that Ruth was not one to be pushed, the Clerk left it at that.

After leaving Ruth's office, Elizabeth remained in the building. She went up to the third floor, determined to meet Louis Lazier. Anyone who had dated Janet commended himself to Elizabeth's attention. But on the stairs she met Forrest Lang, or rather, he met her. He was going in the same direction as the Quaker but moving much more rapidly.

"Excuse me for being so slow," said Elizabeth. As Forrest sidled by her she asked, "Could I speak to you for a minute?"

Forrest slowed but did not stop. "About what?" he asked in a surly voice laced with the Lone Star state.

"About murder," responded Elizabeth.

The student stopped, three steps above. His angular body showed all the tension within it. "Why does our murder matter to you?" he asked.

"I'm concerned about Janet Stevens," said Elizabeth. "She's been under a lot of stress."

"So I gather. And now she's the best murder suspect in the lab."

"Except that she isn't guilty. The question becomes, who is the second best suspect."

"His ex-wife, perhaps. It's more likely her than Eric or me."

"Except, of course, that she wouldn't know how to operate the equipment to release the poison gas," said the Quaker quietly. "It really must be one of you students. Even though Ruth is around here every day, she doesn't know any more than I do about the apparatus. It all looks like science fiction to us."

"No doubt," said Forrest, his self-satisfaction evident. "We do know the lab, of course, but, remember, we look after our own interests. Why would we want to kill Professor Chadwick? His letters of recommendation and his promotion of our careers were worth everything to us. Except for Janet. She blew her chance at a good letter by filing a complaint against him. She's the only possible suspect. She hated him and his death doesn't hurt her career: her chances of a decent postdoc are nil, anyway."

"Why's that?"

"Because everybody in our field knows she's put

in a complaint against a great man. Troublemakers aren't tolerated in labs."

"As I understand it, you aren't the most team-spirited kind of student yourself," said the Quaker.

"Compared to Janet, I'm easy to deal with. Now, if you'll excuse me." Forrest disappeared up the steps, taking them two at a time.

Elizabeth climbed up to the third floor rather slowly. Across the hallway from the stairs a door was open. She looked in and saw two men surrounded by terminals, microscopes, and deep pulsating sounds. Both men were young, although one looked as if he might just be old enough to be a professor.

"Excuse me," said Elizabeth to the room in general. "I'm looking for Louis Lazier."

"I'm Peter Kolakowski," said the nearer man, "but here's Louis." The younger of the two men rose from his stool with a quizzical expression on his face.

"My name is Elizabeth Elliot," said the Quaker to both men and smiled.

Louis came to the door and Elizabeth saw he was good-looking and well built. Janet had had the makings of a fine young man on the line. "What can I do for you?" he asked.

"I happen to be Clerk of the Quaker Meeting just up the street at Longfellow Park. Janet Stevens comes there on Sundays, and yesterday she and I had a long talk. She came to the Meetinghouse looking for help with the situation in this department. I wanted to talk to you, if I could."

"Sure, I'd be glad to," responded Louis earnestly.

"But it can't be this afternoon. I'm taking data now, you see. But tomorrow, anytime is fine."

A time and place for a lunchtime meeting were set. Elizabeth departed with a favorable impression of the man Janet had been dating earlier in the year.

As Elizabeth left the paleontology building, she was glad to escape the sound of compressors and pumps and the harsh fluorescent lighting. She emerged from the building into a much better day. The rain of the night and the wind of the morning were past. March in New England is a fickle month, with spring, summer, and winter all mixed into its thirty-one days.

The Clerk was tired, and she walked leisurely across the grounds of the law school, crossing Massachusetts Avenue above the common. She deliberately avoided the open ground so as not to encounter the homeless who gathered there. She thought about Tim Schouweiler, and she felt her usual worries about him. But, at the moment, she wanted to conserve her emotional strength. Tonight she must clerk the Business Meeting, a gathering that could go past 10 P.M. What remained of the day she resolved to spend at rest.

When she got home, Elizabeth decided to take a nap before addressing supper and going to the Business Meeting. She lay down under the afghan on the living room sofa. Just as she was about to drift off into the haze of a nap, her eyes opened abruptly. She remembered now that John Anderson, the man who had written to the Meeting from Norfolk prison, had been a high school classmate and sometime friend of her son Andrew. That was why the name had seemed so familiar. Last summer, when Andrew had been home for a high school reunion, there had been talk of a classmate in jail. Could it have been for child abuse? Or was it rape? In any event, John Anderson was likely the same young man now writing to Meeting. Considering this, Elizabeth thanked God that her boys had been preserved from John's path. She turned the matter over in her mind until she slept.

The Clerk rose from her sofa at six o'clock, had a piece of reheated pot roast, carrots, and a potato, and went to the Meetinghouse. She arrived twenty minutes early, unlocked the doors, and turned on the lights. Friends soon began to arrive and chat quietly with one another. When Ralph Park appeared, Elizabeth greeted him.

"I got a letter from a local man yesterday. John Anderson is his name," the Clerk began. "He knows of Friends through some work Peace and Social Concerns did in Concord prison a while ago. He wrote to me as Clerk because he's getting out of prison soon and would like us to contact him."

"I was part of the visitation project. I recollect the name," said Ralph, accepting the letter from Elizabeth's hand. "He was a rapist, if I remember rightly. But not a knife-at-your-throat kind of guy. Maybe it was statutory rape he was in for. He was a regular attender of our meetings, I remember that."

"He says he needs a place to stay when he's released. He's told the parole people he can stay with his father, but he says there are family troubles at home. If he's the man I'm thinking of, he was a classmate of my Andrew. He's been to my house, as a child. So you see, I may be called to take a personal interest in this. He could stay with me until he has somewhere to go. Would you think it over and call me?"

Ralph nodded. "But, Friend, even if he's the John Anderson you remember, he'll be different from what he was. You're not cut out to deal with ex-convicts. Their lives are different."

"If I'm called to respond, I'm sure the Lord will lead me in the work," said Elizabeth quietly. "What kind of witness would I be if I didn't meet the needs of one of my boy's childhood friends when he asked the Meeting for help?"

Ralph did not answer but slowly shook his head.

Elizabeth returned to the center of the room to take up her place as Clerk and begin the short period of worship which preceded Business Meeting. Quaker silence began to fill space as Friends settled into prayer. The large room was quickly awash with a sense of calm. Soon Elizabeth felt centered. A few minutes later, when the time was right, she opened the Business Meeting by reading from a guide book to Quaker life, *Faith and Practice of New England Yearly Meeting of Friends*. Elizabeth had chosen a passage on stewardship. She read a quotation from the journals of an eighteenth-century Friend named John Woolman and then waited a moment for the silence to deepen.

"We need to consider a question of stewardship within our Meeting," said Elizabeth. "As we know, access to the Meetinghouse is all but impossible for those Friends and visitors confined to wheelchairs. The Facilities Committee submitted its report last month calling on us to build a ramp for wheelchair access to our building. As you will recall, Friends felt clear to ask the Finance Committee to consider how we might proceed and report to us at this Business Meeting. I call on Hugo Coleman, Clerk of Finance."

Hugo, a man of Elizabeth's generation who had been important to the operations of Business Meeting for years, rose and cleared his throat.

"Friends, we've checked with two contractors to get estimates for a concrete ramp for wheelchair access. There is a maximum grade for these ramps, and that means they are long. Ours would have to be about fifty feet long to get up our steps. Financing is not the chief problem; the estimates are not as high as we had feared."

Elizabeth, who had not spoken to Hugo before the Meeting, was glad to hear this. She disliked money-raising campaigns of all sorts. Because she had anticipated that money would be a problem, she had kept some distance between her Clerkship and this question.

"But a serious question remains," continued Hugo. "Because of the way our lot is shaped, a ramp up to the front door would have to start near the public sidewalk. As one approached the Meetinghouse, a solid concrete ramp is what one would see, with our building, listed in the National Registry of Historical Buildings, behind it."

"Are you saying that the registry prohibits our putting in a handicap ramp?" asked a Friend in the back row.

"No, only that the view from the street would be disfigured." A short silence ensued, broken by the Clerk.

"Perhaps we should think of the look as an inviting one, inviting to all the elderly and handicapped visitors and Friends."

Hugo was still on his feet. He nodded his head toward the Clerk. "Perhaps. Another alternative would be to run the ramp along the back of the building, leading up to the back door. There is length enough for that, and it would not be visible from the street."

Hugo sat down and the room returned to silence. The Clerk was unimpressed. She waited in prayer, hoping another voice might be heard.

Harriet rose to speak. She echoed Hugo's views about aesthetics. Elizabeth prayed more fiercely and was rewarded.

"Friends, we have a simple problem here," said an older woman named Jane Thompson. "Are we going to put the look of our beloved building before the convenience of the people who need a ramp? Perhaps we should be embarrassed for even thinking in these terms." Jane sat down.

Hugo was back on his feet. He pointed out that cars

could drive up to the back of the Meetinghouse. He wondered if people in need of the ramp would not be better off being delivered to it directly from their vehicles. Since there was very limited room behind the Meetinghouse, and it was space that filled instantly on Sundays, the Clerk felt impatient with Hugo. She broke in to ask him a question about the costs the contractors had given and what paying for the ramp, wherever it was located, would do to the budget of the Facilities Committee for the rest of the year.

This topic led the Friends into discussion of financial questions more generally, and an hour passed before the location of the ramp again came to the center of attention. The Clerk, looking at her watch, decided to urge the Meeting to close discussion on the topic for the evening, since there were still several smaller items that needed their attention. Friends concurred, and Business Meeting went on to discuss a problem with the curriculum in the First-day School and the need for more interaction between Quakers and the homeless who came to the Meetinghouse on Sundays.

The Meeting had run its course by 10 P.M. The Clerk was tired and glad to close the session. Neil Stevenson offered to walk home with her through the dark and deserted areas between Longfellow Park and Concord Avenue. He was a shy man and quiet even by Quaker standards. She had been intending to have him over for dinner just before the problems with Janet had arisen and taken her attention. Perhaps she had been putting Neil out of her mind because she feared he would not understand her concerns about

John Anderson. That was a sign, she thought, that she did not yet feel close to him. Nor, she knew, would they ever be any closer if she did not speak about what was on her mind. But it was late and Elizabeth simply did not have the energy to begin a discussion of her present activities. She promised herself she would call Neil and bring him up to date.

Realizing that even a shy man might feel rejected by her silence as they walked, she reached out for his hand in the darkness. He took it and gave it a warm squeeze.

"I've been out of touch, Neil, and I'm sorry for that."

"I've wondered if anything were wrong," said Neil softly.

"No. Things are complicated, at the moment, but not wrong." There was a pause and Elizabeth continued, "I'd like to talk a couple of matters over with you, but tonight doesn't seem the right time. It's so late and clerking these Business Meetings wears me out."

"I know. I can see that from where I sit. You were beginning to droop by the time the Meeting ended. Take your time and call me when you want to talk."

They had reached Elizabeth's house on Concord Avenue. She felt a flash of warmth for this quiet but observant man and happily reached up to his face for a kiss. Then she said good night and let herself into the house.

*   *   *

Patience generally did not attend Business Meeting during the winter months. Walking in the dark on the icy and uneven streets of the neighborhood by the Meetinghouse was risky for her. Knowing that Joel Timmermann would not be at Business Meeting because he only appeared at Meeting on First-days, she called him at home.

"Good evening, Friend," she began. "This is Patience Silverstone. I hope we could speak."

"Certainly," said Joel. "What can I do for you?"

"Perhaps thee could do me the favor of rethinking something thee expressed to our Clerk."

Joel was taken aback. "I'm not sure what you mean," he said warily.

"Sometimes we respond to information without taking time for thought," answered Patience smoothly. "I know most of my actions are based on reflex, not careful examination of an issue."

She paused, but Joel said nothing.

"I'm sure that life at the university has a lot of pressure. Perhaps thee minimizes some kinds of responsibility in order to get work accomplished."

"Would you speak more clearly," said Joel shortly. "I don't understand what you're driving at. Elizabeth called me to ask advice about a student who has been telling her tales. Maybe some of them true—who knows?—but typical student gossip, it seemed to me. I know she was angry by the end of our conversation. But I don't hold myself responsible for that."

"I'm asking thee to reconsider the whole situation.

From a different perspective. Cecilia is still here in Cambridge, isn't she?"

Cecilia was Joel's daughter. She lived with her mother, Joel's former wife.

"Yes, although I can't see what that has to do with anything."

"Is she in high school?"

"She's graduating at the end of this year. She's been accepted on the early admissions system at Princeton." There was an unmistakable note of pride in Joel's voice, although it was quietly expressed.

"It might help to understand our Clerk if thee thought about how Cecilia would respond to unwanted attention from a professor at Princeton," said Patience. "It could happen to her, Friend. No woman is exempt from such experiences. What should the Quaker witness be on such matters?"

There was silence on the line. Patience could not tell if the silence betokened thought on Joel's part or only continued defensiveness.

"Cecilia's behavior might be perfectly correct and proper in every way," Patience continued. "But what if one of her teachers has an illness, a sickness of the sort that leads him to take advantage of his position? Students look up to teachers, remember. Perhaps thee can see how much damage can be done to a young woman if thee thinks about Cecilia and Princeton."

"I don't see the cases as similar," responded Joel. But there was less defensiveness in his tone.

"In a situation where she were the only young woman around, Cecilia might feel terribly alone. Especially if she had to deal with a man like the one at Harvard. She might feel under assault, to use strong words for it. What I hope is that thee might consider what the Clerk was trying to say in that light.

"I appreciate our speaking, Friend," finished Patience. "Good evening."

CHAPTER SIX

I laid me down and slept; I awaked; for the Lord
sustained me.
PSALM 3:5

Arthritic pain greeted Elizabeth when she awoke. Her neck and the fingers in her right hand ached. Without moving, she opened her eyes and looked at her alarm clock. It was 5:45 A.M. After a few minutes of lying still, she gave up the hope of more sleep. She arose and went downstairs. Looking out the window in the front hallway, she saw that it had snowed during the night. At least six inches had fallen. She sighed; it was no wonder that her joints were rebelling.

Sparkle, a calico cat, greeted her in the kitchen and meowed for an early breakfast. She was an indoor animal, but so shy that she lived much of her life outside Elizabeth's view, in the basement. Sparkle had been a half-starved stray eight years ago when Michael Elliot had adopted her. The adoption, Elizabeth believed, had grown out of the loss her husband had felt when the boys had grown up and moved out. Typical of men, especially men of his generation, Michael had not been expressive of his emotions. But adopting a needy animal was not the worst response that could be imagined to the empty-nest syndrome.

Sparkle had remained wary of humans, although it accepted the Elliots' care. Elizabeth had never been enthusiastic about cats, but the calico reminded her of her husband and she was glad to see her each morning. Elizabeth rewarded the cat for its sociability with a bit of tuna.

"It's not easy being stiff, is it Sparkle?" said Elizabeth as she stroked the animal. For an instant the cat purred, and it was the Quaker's turn to be rewarded.

Elizabeth breakfasted and took her blood pressure and arthritis medicines for the morning. Then, with a heating pad on her neck, she curled up on the living room sofa and listened to classical music and the news on National Public Radio. By 7:00 A.M. she was feeling a little better. She stretched her neck carefully, rubbing the tender vertebrae with her left hand. The pains in the fingers of her right hand were much more bearable than when she had awakened. With a sigh, she went upstairs to dress and officially begin the day.

Returning downstairs, she made a pot of tea and began to work on a draft of the State of the Society report. It was due in the summer at New England Yearly Meeting, an annual event which brought Quakers from half a dozen states together to sojourn and talk. Elizabeth began the report with comments on the slow but significant growth in membership that the group was enjoying. Friends, never inclined to evangelize, had reason to rejoice when new persons made their way to Meeting. Next she addressed more difficult matters. An hour and then another passed. She was just finishing a long paragraph concerning her Meeting's failure to make the homeless feel welcome on Sundays, when the phone rang.

"Mrs. Elliot, I hope I'm not calling too early," began Janet.

"Not at all! What can I do for you?"

"I've come to a decision. I've been terribly depressed for a long time. But all that is changing now. It seems awful to say, but a real weight has been lifted from me. I know I'm terribly angry about everything, but I'm getting my act together and I want to stay in school. I'll do my thesis and show those asses in my department that my research has been top-notch stuff. I could be finished with school by next fall and then go on to a postdoc somewhere else. I know that, if the police suspect me of murder, the same might be true of the department and even the administration. I know it will be hard, but I'm not going to drop out now!"

Elizabeth was delighted to hear the change in Janet's voice. Her thoughts about the future sounded ambitious, but the important thing, from the Quaker's perspective, was that the young woman was forming plans. "Your thesis evaluation will be complicated by your old situation with Professor Chadwick and by his death, too. But, still, writing a thesis is what you have to do now, and I'm sure the department has the ability to respond professionally to the situation. The chairman—Professor Scott, is it?—will likely want to minimize any trouble he can; low-level administrators tend to think like that," said Elizabeth meditatively.

"I'm not thinking of minimizing anything, Mrs. Elliot. I want to continue with the complaint I filed. Chadwick is dead, of course, so he can't hurt anyone else, but he did hurt me and the university should formally recognize that. I'm not sure if they will, or if they'll just declare everything moot."

"I didn't mean to say you should minimize the wrong done to you. Far from it. I was just trying to look at this from the university's perspective for a moment. Is there one of the deans whom you could speak with to sound out what the authorities are thinking about the complaint now?"

"Yes. As it happens, I have an appointment with the assistant dean of the graduate school, Dean North. It's an appointment left over from before the murder. It was to discuss the next step in the formal complaint. Dean North has always been good about explaining my rights. I'll keep the appointment; I want to know what rights I still have. What that man did to me was wrong!

"I can see everything more clearly now! Since I'm staying in school, I need to know how I can go about getting a new advisor who is competent to understand my work. Paul Chadwick, you see, was the only professor in the department who did my kind of research. That's true for the men, too. But I suppose Peter Kolakowski could step in for purposes of signing our completed theses. And a professor at MIT named Judson could be a good advisor as I finish up. Whatever the department will be doing for the men is OK for me, too, but I know the chairman won't think about me unless prodded. He only views me as a problem. The deans may have to remind him I deserve equal treatment."

Janet paused, then said hesitantly, "I know it's a lot to ask, but I was wondering if you could come with me to my appointment. It's half an hour from now. I'm so angry now I get a little afraid of myself, sometimes. I don't want to yell at the deans, especially Dean North. She really has been kind. Could you come along with me for moral support? Maybe your presence would help keep me on an even keel."

"I'll be glad to come," answered Elizabeth without hesitation. "Where on campus shall I meet you?"

Janet explained the location of Byerly Hall, and she and Elizabeth hung up.

The Clerk saw she did not have much time. She put away the State of the Society draft and tugged on her high brown snow boots. She left the house by the back door, filling the bird feeders with seed in passing. She then walked slowly around the house through the heavy, wet snow. Most of the sidewalks along Concord Avenue were not shoveled, as usual. The street was far too busy to walk in. It was easy to criticize the management of the apartment buildings on the avenue for failing to clear their walks, but because her own sidewalk had not been regularly shoveled since her husband's death, Elizabeth counseled herself to take the beam out of her own eye before criticizing her neighbors. Still, walking through the slop was not easy, and she made the trip slowly. She revived a bit during the brief rests at street corners which the heavy traffic necessitated.

Byerly Hall, next to Christ Church on Garden Street, was easy to find. Elizabeth went in the main door from Radcliffe Yard and immediately saw Janet.

"Thanks for coming! I'm glad for your company."

Elizabeth again expressed her willingness to be of any use she could. She was beginning to agree with Ruth that Janet had the right combination of traits to be a powerful force for good in the world someday. But at present, especially by the Clerk's standards, she was still a raw youth, and she was more volatile than a Quaker should be.

"Dean North's office is just up these stairs," said Janet, leading the way. "She's a good sort, as deans go. I think she's the only person here who gives a shit about us students. Sorry about my language! I wasn't thinking."

"It's all right," replied the Clerk. "I've heard the word before."

Dean North was in and ready to see them. They entered a small office overlooking Garden Street. The dean smiled at Janet, accepted her statement that Elizabeth had come along for moral support, and invited both women to sit down.

"Yesterday I realized that I can go back to the labs, now that Professor Chadwick is gone. It sounds pretty terrible, maybe, but I feel much better about work now that I know I won't meet him. I need to have a new advisor assigned to me. I think it should be Peter

Kolakowski, even though what I do is not really his strong suit, or Wally Judson at MIT. My work is almost finished and I'd hope to leave in the fall semester."

"Good," responded the dean. Her eyes searched Janet's face just as they had when the two met on the coldest day of February. "We want you to continue. Your education has been disrupted, long before this tragic death, through no fault of your own. You have a right to finish your degree. Officially, the university takes no position on the death of Professor Chadwick. But let me assure you that my office is behind you one hundred percent."

"Thank you," said Janet. Tears crept into her eyes. Elizabeth handed Janet her lace-edged hanky, and the young woman dabbed at her face. "I'll be glad to get back to the science I was doing. Research has meant the world to me these past few years, and I want to continue.

"But on a more important topic, I think the university should still consider the complaint I made. I know that Chadwick is dead and can't hurt anyone else, but I think Harvard should admit what has been wrong in that department."

"I can understand your concern," said the dean in a more reserved tone. "We have few written complaints about harassment problems. We've never had the object of the complaint die just as the university's process of investigation was beginning. I can't say exactly what will happen, but I can assure you that you have already accomplished a great deal. By coming forward, you have made a difference. For the whole university."

Janet shook her head, unwilling to be put off by praise. "The chairman should apologize to me for what he said. And the other men. They said it was my fault, that I wasn't strong, that I let him treat me that way. They said I was making a mountain out of a molehill, that I was exaggerating! They said all kinds of things!"

"I'm sorry about your experiences at Harvard," said Dean North. "We in the administration regret them deeply. I'm afraid most of the men on the faculty don't understand the concept of apology. But I hope you'll believe that I'm sorry for all that occurred in that laboratory."

"Yes, I'm sure you are," said Janet, again close to tears. "And thanks for saying so. But you're a woman, and you're not on the faculty. They need to see the wrong they did, not you!"

"Perhaps the most difficult part of the original problem," said Elizabeth, "is understanding the attitudes of the other men in the department. Why was Professor Chadwick's behavior tolerated?"

"The senior faculty are a mystery in several respects," said the dean, shaking her head.

"A mystery with nefarious consequences for some," said Elizabeth.

"Absolutely," said Dean North. "I am sorry," she repeated. "But what happens now about the complaint is up to the senior deans, Robert Williams in particular. And I don't expect the university will want to continue an investigation now that the object of the complaint has been removed from the scene. Furthermore, Janet, although I do believe in you, you must realize that you are skating on thin ice. No one else has come forward with your type of story about Paul Chadwick, you know."

"But all the other students are men!" cried Janet indignantly, half rising from her chair. "Of course they don't have those problems!"

"And then there's the problem of the murder," continued Dean North, no longer looking directly at Janet. "The other deans don't know you as I do. They will certainly have to consider you as a murder suspect. So tread lightly, that's my best advice to you, and get your degree as quietly as possible."

Janet saw that there was nothing more to be hoped for. She stood up stiffly and looked at Elizabeth. Against her will, the student thanked the dean for her time. Elizabeth nodded respectfully at Dean North and stepped out the office door after Janet.

The two women walked slowly through the melting snow to Janet's dormitory.

As they crossed Massachusetts Avenue and entered Harvard Yard, Janet exploded. "I'll sue them all! They want to get out of this now that that man is dead. But I'm not done! It was wrong, and I'm going to sue! Eric's wife said to me the trouble was that I didn't protect myself. She's an MBA, and she has to work with lots of men, I'm sure. She said I needed to take self-defense classes to build up self-confidence. And that I should learn how to be nasty, just with words, and always be on my guard. But why should I have to change so much when all I wanted to do was study? I don't want to take karate! I have a right to be at this school! I shouldn't have to defend myself from slime every day in the labs."

The two women emerged from the Yard onto Oxford Street as Janet continued, "It's not up to us victims always to defend ourselves. I mean, I see the point that I could have done more, but that wasn't the real problem. The problem was the way that man behaved! And the way all the other men tolerated it! Well, I'm mad now, and now I'll defend myself. I'll sue, by God!"

"It was very wrong, what you experienced," said Elizabeth, "and I agree that the innocent often are blamed for not 'defending' themselves. It's convenient for the world to look at things that way. But, just as a practical point, lawsuits don't always have much to do with what's right and what's wrong. You may have grounds to sue, and you may not. The law is peculiar."

"I don't care! I'll write a book, then, and expose them all for what they are! Especially Dean North!"

Elizabeth smiled slightly. "She didn't tell you the trouble was that you asked for it or that you didn't defend yourself. And she clearly does want you to get your degree."

"Yes, she wants that. But if I pursue the complaint, she's telling me I'll be a murder suspect in everyone's eyes. And if I drop the complaint, the deans will be nice to me."

"What she said was maybe a little bit different," responded the mature Quaker. "Like me, she thinks the murder may affect everybody in the department, more than you know at present. You are a bit angry, Friend."

"Thanks for calling me that," said Janet more calmly. "I know I'm angry. But there's good reason!"

"Indeed," said Elizabeth, "I've not lost sight of that."

When they arrived at Janet's dorm, Elizabeth stepped inside the main doors of the building but explained she could not stay. She said she had a lunch date in the Square. Because she did not yet understand the present situation between Janet and Louis, she did not explain whom she was going to meet nor ask Janet along. Elizabeth reminded Janet of her two o'clock appointment with Doug Gibson and volunteered to come with Janet to Gibson's office.

"I could manage by myself, I think," said Janet.

"I'm sure that's true. But I'd like to come along and hear what the lawyer has to say."

"I'll ask him if I have grounds to sue," said Janet meditatively.

"First things first! You are a suspect for murder! Let me come with you, and see if I can be helpful."

"OK," said Janet, "that would be fine."

"Let's meet at the subway stop in the Square at one thirty," responded Elizabeth quickly.

As the Clerk left, she was glad to see Janet run up the stairs. The student was on the road to recovery, it seemed, but it was healing fueled at present by tremendous anger. She hoped that Janet would do nothing reckless while her emotions were so extreme.

Elizabeth arrived at the Stockpot restaurant in Harvard Square at noon. Louis Lazier was waiting for her.

"Hi, Mrs. Elliot," said the good-looking young man with real cheer.

"Thanks for coming through all this snow," said the Quaker, smiling.

"It's no problem. Janet means a lot to me, even though we've been out of touch." Louis blushed slightly but continued. "Sometimes it seems like she's angry with everyone in our department, including me. That's hard because I've always tried to be helpful. I'm afraid we had some harsh words on the subject just before she went to the deans. It would have blown over, I'm sure, but she hasn't been back to work, and she's not answered the messages I've left for her. So I'm glad to talk to anyone who is being helpful to her."

After the pair got a table and ordered soup and sandwiches, Elizabeth cleared her throat and began in a serious tone, "I don't really know Janet, but I'm concerned about her. She's been coming to the Meetinghouse up the street where I'm Clerk. I didn't speak with her until Monday when she showed up at our building. She was deeply hurt and distressed. That was before we knew about Professor Chadwick's death."

"Professors like him are a great problem in science," said Louis. "In the humanities, if there is personal trouble, students can get away from a guy more easily by changing their major professor. But someone in Janet's position has to get along with her advisor. She has to work in his lab, use the equipment that belongs to him. Her paycheck comes from his grants. Her publications will have his name on them as a co-author. Or, knowing Chadwick, if she's not careful, her name might not appear at all on her own work! Anyway, if there's a sicko in our department, it was Paul Chadwick. No women should have been allowed to work with him."

"If the department understands the problem, why didn't anyone do something?" asked Elizabeth, suppressing her indignation as best she could.

"Partly because the senior faculty are cowards. But mostly because they're selfish. It would take time and energy to respond to the situation. If they just ignore it, they can get on with their own work. What happens within Chadwick's lab isn't their responsibility."

"But surely the department does have a responsibility to let women students get an education without being attacked!"

"You don't need to convince me. But I'm just a student. There wasn't anything I could do except to listen to Janet and try to be supportive."

"Janet has told me you've been helpful," said Elizabeth with a nod. "I apologize if I seemed angry with you. Clearly it's the faculty and the chairman I need to address. Anyway, I'm happy to report that Janet is perking up rapidly now, although she's becoming more and more angry as she sees what's been done to her. But I expect she'll be back in your lab building soon. Of course, there's now the enormous complication of her being a murder suspect."

Elizabeth paused for a moment. "I know it's an awkward thing to think about, but can you tell me who had access to the lab? Who would have understood enough of the apparatus to gas Professor Chadwick?"

Louis thought for a moment before replying. "Basically, all of us. All the graduate students know the lab well. We pretty much live there, after all. And I don't know how you could eliminate anybody in terms of time, because the police were asking us about a long period—all day Sunday and Sunday night. Any of us could have come in, whatever we might say about where we were. We all have keys. We all could have done it."

"But the killer must have known Chadwick's schedule—known when he would be in the laboratory." Elizabeth frowned as she considered the possibility that Chadwick had not been the intended victim. She shook her head. "Ruth told me you were at work on Sunday. Did you see anyone else?"

"No, and that's a little unfortunate. I told the police I'd been there all day, and that's the truth, but no one came up to our floor. My lab is on the third floor, you see. Chadwick and his students are on the second. I'm a little afraid that the detective who interviewed me thinks it's odd I could have been there all day Sunday without being seen by a soul."

"Your advisor doesn't work on Sundays, I take it."

"Actually he usually does. I'm the one who's generally not around on Sundays. I like to go to mass in the morning and watch football or baseball in the afternoon. But I went in because I fell behind on a deadline, and I had a lot to finish up. Normally Peter Kolakowski, my advisor, would have been there. Professors without tenure work seven days a week, pretty much. But he was out of town. He flew down to New York on the early-morning shuttle on Sunday. His parents live there. He flew back on Monday morning. Anyway, that's what he told me, and I'm sure that's right. He goes down to 'the City' on Sundays every month or so. The police can easily check with the airlines. So anyway, with him not around, there was no one on the third floor but me.

"But to get back to my point, even though lots of people have the opportunity to mess with the oxygen line and somehow make the chlorine pentafluoride escape, I can't see why any of us would. Even though Chadwick was a jerk about acknowledging ideas and about women, we don't have a motive for murder! Chadwick's students, even Janet, lose a lot because of his death."

"But it apparently wasn't an accident," murmured the Quaker. "The police seem certain about that. If it wasn't Janet, it must have been someone else in the lab. What do you think of Forrest Lang? I met him and he seems to have plenty of hostility. I take it he and Chadwick didn't get along."

"No. Forrest doesn't get along with anybody, as far as I can tell. And Chadwick could be hard to deal with. My advisor isn't like that at all, but old professors are asses a lot of the time. Harvard goes to their heads. Forrest was around early on Sunday, I think, because I saw his bike locked up on the north side of the building. He bought it from me, you see. It's my old bike and it's impossible for me not to notice it."

"Did you see him inside the building?"

"No. But I wasn't on the second floor."

The waitress brought their food. Elizabeth paused briefly in silence.

"I gather Eric is almost done," said Elizabeth easily when she was finished with prayer.

"Yes. He can leave anytime he gets a postdoc lined up. He's got two articles in print. It was going to be three, the third one being some additional work he did here continuing his senior thesis research at Princeton. But he dropped that in the fall; I'm not sure why. Still, publishing two good articles is fine, and his really are good.

"There's been a lot of stress on him this year. Writing articles is quite a chore, the first time you do it. And he's had bad luck. He told me just recently his funding for this semester was messed up, but I don't know why. So he's had to be a teaching assistant in a big undergraduate course. It pays more than you might think, but it takes up a lot of time. But his research work really is pretty much complete. It's a shame he's had to waste his time teaching. I'm sure he'll be glad to get out, especially now.

"And Forrest Lang's not far behind. He's got his results now, from what I can tell. Forrest is secretive—it's sort of a joke. He asks me a lot of questions about what I'm doing, but he'll never answer about his own stuff. But I know he's basically done because Professor Chadwick told me so just a little while ago. Forrest'll write everything up in a fury and get out quick, I'm sure."

"Where are you from?" asked Elizabeth on impulse. Louis's accent was clearly not that of New England.

"From Manhattan. I think Boston is a sleepy little town," he said with a smile, "but I like it."

Elizabeth smiled, too. Boston was still the big city to her. Cambridge was her preference, because it was built on a more modest and comprehensible scale. She had not been to New York for almost twenty years and could not imagine living there.

"Do the professors in your department get along?"

"No. But Harvard professors aren't known for getting along with each other. My advisor has raised some hackles with the old farts. He's an easygoing guy, but he's put out so many articles in the past five years that they just can't keep up. And the grant money is flowing to him, the way it always does when you publish."

"What makes his productivity so high?"

"To tell you the truth, I've wondered about that," answered the student stiffly. He paused in thought and then continued. "He's smart, but so are the rest of us. He's driven, but that's not unusual. He does do lab work, which is sort of unusual for a professor. But how he gets all his data in so quickly is something I haven't figured out. He says he pulls all-nighters."

Elizabeth considered this. Working all night still did not seem an efficient way of getting things accomplished. The fatigue the following day would make more progress next to impossible.

"Janet tells me there's been some trouble with Professor Chadwick over who should be given credit for ideas he used. You probably know those stories."

Louis nodded his head.

The Quaker continued: "I saw a science program recently on WGBH. It said that the pressure to get more funding is intense. In a number of cases, scientists have committed fraud, just from the supercompetitive atmosphere—falsifying data, making up results, and so forth." Elizabeth paused and looked at Louis. "Did you happen to see that show?"

"No," answered the graduate student. "We don't have a TV in the lab, and I live at work, I'm afraid. I know some cases of cheating in cancer research. That's very different from the acknowledgment problem, which is what Paul Chadwick was known for. He had a knack for taking pieces of an idea from someone else and not giving them credit."

"Yes," said Elizabeth quickly. "I can see that's a different issue. The program I mentioned discussed greater transgressions. It used the controversy about the discovery of the AIDS virus as an example of

what competition can lead to, with two groups claiming to be first, even though one may have borrowed
the cultured virus from the other's lab. That's an extreme case. The problem of acknowledging everybody
who should be acknowledged must be more common.
May I ask, has your advisor had some of those con-
troversies too?"

"No," said Louis. "He works more in his own little
area. There aren't people to compete with in such a
direct way as for Chadwick. My advisor isn't a the-
orist or a great thinker, but he has produced a lot of
data, all of it answering important questions. His data
don't infringe on other people's work."

Louis looked at his watch and said that he had to
be getting back to his laboratory. Elizabeth nodded.

"It's not my business, of course, and I hope you'll
forgive me for mentioning it, but from what I know,
I think Janet would be glad if you looked her up
again. She must have been deeply distressed just before she ran away from Chadwick, and if harsh words
passed between you two they may well have sprung
from her feelings about him, not you. But forgive me
if I've been inappropriate."

"Not at all," responded Louis with a quick smile.
"I'm glad to know. And thanks for looking me up
yesterday; it's been good to talk to you."

Louis reached for his wallet and Elizabeth for her
purse. They divided the bill between them.

*   *   *

Elizabeth waited for Janet near the information booth at the top of the subway stairs, as the two women had agreed. Soon the graduate student came into view, and they caught the subway together. The Quaker was glad to see that the young woman was much calmer than she had been in the morning. The subway's screeches, clangs, and bumps between Harvard Square and Central Square were extreme, as usual, but they eventually emerged up a stairway into the daylight again and easily found Douglas Gibson's office. He was a partner in a firm specializing in criminal law. The offices the two women entered were not posh, but the place was busy, which Elizabeth thought was a good sign. A secretary invited them to wait in a cubbyhole at the end of the corridor, promising that Mr. Gibson would soon appear. He did.

"I'm glad to see you both again," began the lawyer briskly, not giving the women time to speak. "I've had a look at the pathologist's report now, and I understand what's in Burnham's mind. Paul Chadwick died from inhaling a corrosive and toxic gas. That's clear. The identity of the gas can't be known for certain, but the way it acted within his body is consistent with the properties of chlorine pentafluoride. And the key point about the oxygen line," said the lawyer frowning, "is that it holds that gas and could release it."

Janet nodded. "But the line would release the gas only if you did a couple of stupid things while working with it. You'd have to open three valves in a row. It's designed to not happen accidentally."

"And those valves could have been operated on timers?" asked Gibson.

"No. Only the last one could. The first two are completely manual. Unless you rebuilt them, somebody would have to be there to open them by hand."

"But they could be opened by hand, and then the third one opened automatically sometime later?"

"That's right," said Janet slowly, clearly not used to thinking of the apparatus in this light.

"Who uses the equipment on a day-to-day basis?"

"It's only used now and then, but it's used by everybody in the building except for my advisor, who was too old to do any real work, and the secretaries, and the chairman down on the first floor."

"Did the police take your fingerprints?" asked the attorney.

"No."

"They will. Don't get alarmed. Your prints had a right to be all over the laboratory, didn't they?"

"Sure, I've worked there for years."

"What we should do for now, is line up the people who know where you were on Sunday. Even though it doesn't cover all the time in question—which is three to six P.M. on Sunday, from what Burnham tells me about the presumed time of death—I'll get affidavits from the students you were with. Would you write down their names for me here? I'll get in touch with them tomorrow morning before their memories of Sunday fade further. For now, that's all we can do. We'll see what the police pursue. Remember, they have the burden of proof. You have a motive, perhaps, but many people seem to have had opportunity galore. Even if you're charged, there's a good chance we can win in court."

"Let's not consider that," said Elizabeth hastily. "Someone else did set up the oxygen line to kill. All we need do is find out how that happened. The murderer may have been seen by someone. It's a busy building, after all."

"Yes, Mrs. Elliot, that would be convenient. But we can hardly count on it, so I'll do what I can with the affidavits."

"I don't think that Sunday during the daytime can be terribly important," said Janet thoughtfully. "No one would risk setting up timers then, when anybody could pop into the lab at any moment. If the line was rigged to kill, the job of setting it up would have been done at night. That means Saturday night. I can check with the weekend security man, Jack somebody-or-other. The killer must have known when Chadwick would be in that lab. He set the timer for that period." Janet paused and then said almost to herself, "Who would know Paul's schedule for the weekend?"

Elizabeth was glad to see the young woman was thinking critically and calmly. But she suspected that the student's strong emotions were just beneath the surface. As if on cue, Janet cleared her throat and continued.

"I'm not sure you're the right kind of lawyer, Mr. Gibson, but I want to know if I can sue my department for tolerating the harassment I experienced for so long."

Doug Gibson was startled. He looked at Janet for a moment before replying.

"I'm not a litigation lawyer, but I know it's extraordinarily difficult to prove harassment. And the burden of proof would be on you. You would have to sue the university, not your department, and Harvard has many excellent lawyers on its staff who will cheerfully work against you. Their first job would be to delay the proceedings, something we lawyers do quite well. You might find a lawyer who would take the case on contingency, meaning you wouldn't have to pay his salary up-front, but you would be responsible for court costs. And federal law has not been generous to women claiming harassment as a type of discrimination, which is what your case would amount to."

"Is the law in Massachusetts any better?" asked Janet.

Again, Gibson was startled. "You're quick," he said. "You should consider going into the law yourself! The honest answer is that I don't know the Commonwealth's laws for gender-based suits. But I'll check with one of my colleagues who would know. Is that enough for the present?"

"Yes," replied Janet. She forced herself to smile.

"The murder case, I would say, is a much more serious legal matter. You may have to deal with it, whether you wish to or not. Please do check with the security man in your building about Saturday night. Call me. Meanwhile, I'll gather affidavits from your dorm mates."

Elizabeth was glad the lawyer thought there was something constructive he could do, but she also thought a lot more than affidavits would be necessary to help Janet Stevens. With Burnham's suspicions focused on Janet, Elizabeth resolved to do all she could to find a solution to the crime. As they left the lawyer's office, Elizabeth invited Janet to lunch the next day at her house. Janet thanked her for the invitation and accepted readily.

"I'm glad to be with someone as calm as you, Mrs. Elliot. I feel like a stranger to myself; I've never felt so enraged. Thanks for putting up with me."

Elizabeth returned home and rested for a while at the kitchen table, but a Clerk's work is never done, so she found herself all too soon dialing Ralph Park's telephone number. They discussed John Anderson's request for a place to stay when he was released. Ralph again said that Elizabeth did not know the young man, especially as he now was.

"Yes, but I'd like to speak to him," said the Clerk. "That might help me. I can remember him here in the backyard, playing after school when the boys were little. Can I visit him at Concord?"

"Yes, although it's not a minor undertaking. You might have to submit to a body search. That includes an examination of body cavities. Need I say more? But you don't have to do a prison visit just to speak to him. Anderson can call you. At Concord, they have access to phones. Should I give him your number?"

"Yes, please."

"A great deal can change in a person over the years," said Ralph carefully. "Even though this is the same fellow your son knew, remember that he's spent several years in jails and prisons. He's been learning a lot, you may be sure."

"I understand that," replied the Clerk firmly. "I feel clear about this and I'd like him to call if he wishes."

Elizabeth and Ralph said good-bye and, after brewing herself a small pot of English breakfast tea, she again sat down at the kitchen table. The Clerk took up the newspaper she had bought while returning from Harvard Square. She was shocked and saddened to see on the front page a story about two killings, one in the subway between Boston and MIT, one just beside a subway entrance stairwell. For the first time, Elizabeth began to wonder what crimes John had committed. She remembered at Business Meeting Ralph had said he had not been terribly violent. But if it were rape he'd been found guilty of, that was necessarily violent, was it not? Except for statutory rape. Elizabeth wondered where the Commonwealth of Massachusetts drew the age line for sex between a minor and an adult, at eighteen or sixteen? And then there was "date rape," a term with which Elizabeth was barely familiar. If it meant what she thought it did, that was surely a form of violence, too. Still, she reminded herself, she had felt clear about asking John to contact her and she had to do that to which she had now committed herself.

*   *   *

The evening of the same day, after receiving a cheering phone call from Louis, Janet Stevens decided to try to reach the weekend security man who worked in the paleontology building at the university. She left her dorm and walked across Oxford Street. She was pleased to note that she no longer felt ashamed at the thought of entering her building and walking around the labs. At least the worst part of the injury of the past was dropping away.

Janet let herself in the main doors and slowly walked through the hallways of the first floor. No one at all was around. She went up to the second floor and chatted awkwardly with Eric, who was finishing up something in the lab, and then walked up to the third floor. There she found the nighttime security man who worked during the week. He was sitting beside one of the large cabinets in the hall, drinking something from a thermos and listening to a small radio.

"Hi, Bob," she said with a smile.

"I'll have to see some ID, young lady. It's been so long since I've seen you I'm not sure if you belong here!"

Janet laughed. "Yup, it's me all right. And I'm back to stay. I'm not going to let the bastards get me down anymore. How have you been?"

"Same as always. Since the professor was found dead there's been a shake-up for us, I can tell you. I now have to spend half the night here, before walking through my other buildings. Kind of locking the barn doors after the horse has been stolen, if you ask me."

"It sounds that way. I want to speak to Jack, the weekend man, and I was wondering if you could tell me where I could find him."

"I don't know his home number. I don't know him, you see, because we don't overlap during the week. In the morning you could call the security office and they'll tell a sweet thing like you whatever you want to know."

Janet felt annoyed but let the remark pass. She was intent on fighting bigger men than Bob and needed to keep focused on what was important. "Do you know his last name? I should know it, but I've forgotten."

"It's Jack Martin," said Bob.

Janet thanked him and went back to her dorm. A little bit of shame was within her, she noticed, as she crossed Oxford Street. The laboratory building, or perhaps Bob, had reminded her of her old predicament.

CHAPTER SEVEN

Behold, the Lord's hand is not shortened, that it cannot save.
ISAIAH 59:1

Louis smiled when he saw Janet on the subway platform the next morning. He waved, and she waved back. As he drew near she returned his smile, then looked away in embarrassment.

"It was nice of you to suggest this trip to the museum. I'm sorry we got stuck at a nasty point a few weeks ago."

"I meant to stop by your dorm and I'm really sorry I didn't. But I thought you needed to work things out on your own. And I thought you'd show up in lab soon, and then we could talk."

"I didn't want to see anybody from the department, not even you. But I'm feeling much more normal. Angry, maybe, but not so ashamed. It's too bad that a death can make you feel so much better."

"Be careful who you say that to. I can understand what you mean, but a lot of people wouldn't."

"You're right," Janet said, looking at Louis with a

fresh smile. "But it's great to know that you understand. And I think Mrs. Elliot does, too."

"Who is this Elizabeth Elliot?" asked Louis.

"She's a Quaker woman from the Meeting here who's being helpful to me."

"But what's her percentage?"

Janet looked disconcerted. She shrugged and replied, "I think Quakers aren't into percentages. I went to a Friends' school as a kid, and I've known Quakers off and on for a long time. They can be sort of different from normal people," replied Janet in an increasingly louder voice as a subway car pulled into the Harvard Square station.

Louis bellowed back, "Let's not talk about any of this anymore! We're off to see the classic works of Western art!" The train stopped. "Paint dripped randomly on the canvases, if we're lucky!" said Louis as he motioned Janet in front of him through the subway doors.

During the screeching and jolting ride between Harvard and Central squares, the two students found it easiest to keep silent. But after Central, as the Red Line straightened out, Louis talked into Janet's ear about the Impressionist paintings at the Boston Museum of Fine Art. By the time the couple changed trains for the Green Line at Park Street, Louis was deep into a lecture about the different periods in Monet's working life.

"The grain stack paintings really marked a change for him," said Louis. Janet looked puzzled. "Those are the ones that Americans call the haystack paintings," explained Louis.

Janet nodded. "Where did you pick all this up?" she asked.

"My mother was in art history in school. She always took us kids to the major museums as part of summer vacation, and beat a lot of things into our thick heads. At the time, we didn't know it was unusual for grade-schoolers to be learning the stuff. But I'm glad for it now. I've been a member of the Museum of Fine Art since coming here. I go down every week or two, just to get away from Harvard shittiness, and spend a couple of hours in one room or another, taking it all in."

"You never mentioned this before! I didn't know there was anybody in our department who appreciated art," said Janet. "All you men talk about at lunch is the Red Sox, and when we were dating, you only wanted to go to movies!"

"That's true, I guess," said Louis. "You won't tell the others about my thoughtful and sensitive side, will you?"

Janet laughed. "Not likely. And I'll be glad to have you as a guide today. I don't know anything about art."

The Green Line tram stopped, and the two students got out. Louis looked at his companion with his old fondness as they crossed Commonwealth Avenue toward the museum.

After a squabble about who should pay for Janet's ticket, which the young woman won, the pair went upstairs to the Impressionist paintings. Louis explained what he knew of the different painters' styles and Janet was glad to listen. He was a good teacher. Next they went to the special exhibit section of the museum, which was showing nudes of a well-known Los Angeles painter.

Janet began to feel uncomfortable within minutes of entering the special exhibit. The nudes were all women and the paintings realistic with grotesque distortions of parts of the female anatomy. By the time she had seen the sixth figure of a woman depicted as a bizarre freak, Janet wanted to go home and told her companion so.

"But there are at least a dozen more," said Louis with a frown.

"They're sick!" said Janet looking away. "The painter is a pervert."

"It's artistic license,"

"You go look at the rest. I'm done," said Janet angrily.

Louis did so. He spent another twenty minutes in the special exhibition rooms while Janet waited at the door. When he returned to her she asked, "Were any of the other paintings male figures?"

"No."

"Exactly! He only shows women distorted like that! Not what's between his own legs!"

Louis considered. He did not think the paintings were out of line for avant garde art, but he did see Janet's point.

"Maybe you're right. Can I buy you a cup of coffee

in the café downstairs? Then, if you'd like, we could look at some of the older things. There's a wonderful collection of medieval tapestries here."

Janet accepted her friend's well-intentioned diversion.

Elizabeth Elliot brewed Darjeeling tea in her favorite teapot and sat down at her table with the State of the Society report. Despite her favorite source of caffeine, she made little progress in her writing, feeling suddenly unsure what the document should cover. The growing problems of the homeless around the Meetinghouse weighed heavily on her heart, but the Clerk was uncertain if most Friends would accept a detailed examination of that situation as an integral part of their corporate life.

Sparkle appeared and, uncharacteristically friendly, seated herself on the chair beside her mistress.

"I'm not sure I was meant to be Clerk," mused Elizabeth to the cat.

The ringing of the telephone sent Sparkle running for the basement. It was Ruth Markham.

"I'm calling to chat on my coffee break," began Ruth. "What's happening with the police? They've not been here for a couple of days. Is Janet still under suspicion, do you think?"

"I'm afraid so," answered Elizabeth. "Douglas Gibson, Janet's lawyer, called me this morning. He spoke to Detective Burnham today. The detective and his assistants have not been able to follow up their work at Harvard lately. They've been putting in a lot of time on those subway killings near MIT."

"I saw them in the paper," said Ruth. "Quite dreadful. But if the Cambridge police know what's good for them, they won't let the murder of a famous Harvard professor go unsolved. The *Globe* has been running a story on Paul Chadwick's death every day! Janet may be the best scapegoat they can find."

"You're always more cynical than I am, Friend. If you're right, we can only hope the murderer is identified by someone or that he comes forward himself. Or I guess I should say himself or herself, not to be so sexist."

"Comes forward!" snorted Ruth, ignoring the last idea. "You expect him to come forward! We're dealing with Harvard faculty and students! These aren't people who are overwhelmed with grief at their transgressions."

"I'm sure that while there is breath, there is hope."

"Don't quote things at me," said Ruth in a bitter tone. "It's pointless." She paused to enjoy her own unhappiness.

Elizabeth followed up an idea she had had during the night. "Do you have records of the chemicals purchased by Professor Chadwick's lab?"

"Certainly. The university's purchase order form is in triplicate. I get the third copy of all orders as they go out, and then I get a photocopy of packing slips when the stuff arrives."

"Could you tell me how many canisters of the chlo-

rine gas—the one with the long name—Chadwick or
his students ordered this year? I'm curious as to how
much should have been on hand in the laboratory."

"Just sit tight," said Ruth. In less than a minute,
she returned.

"Got it! What organized files I have, if I may say
so. They don't deserve me around here. The answer
is: two canisters, purchased last October. Nothing else
for the previous two years. I guess they don't use
much of this stuff."

"Thank you, that may be helpful. How about the
timers that Eric mentioned? And the valves? Do you
have any records of new timers and valves being purchased?"

Ruth sighed. "That will be a little harder to say,
since I don't know the company names. But let me
look."

There was a much longer pause. Elizabeth heard
file drawers slamming. More silence followed. Eventually Ruth returned to the line.

"You still there?" she asked crossly.

"Yes."

"You won't like the answer. Two valves of some
sort and two timers were purchased in early Decem
ber. They were ordered by Janet Stevens."

"Oh, dear."

"Well, you asked," said Ruth hotly.

"Of course I did. I'll be talking to Janet today, and
I'll ask what became of those things after they arrived.
I've invited her over to lunch."

There were sounds over the phone line of a door

opening and closing. "I've got to go," said Ruth abruptly, and the two women hung up.

Janet had called Elizabeth and asked if Louis might come to lunch as well. She explained that they were both in Boston, at the Museum of Fine Arts, and if it wouldn't be inconvenient, Louis would be happy to come with her to Concord Avenue for a home-cooked meal.

The two students arrived at the Quaker's house and Elizabeth welcomed them into the living room. She explained that the chicken pot pie she'd made for lunch needed a few more minutes in the oven and offered them apple cider to hold them over.

"I found out the full name of the weekend security man—Jack Martin," said Janet after finishing her cider. "I got his home number early this morning from the security office and called him. I thought an early-morning call would be better for someone working the night shift than a phone call in the middle of the day."

"That's true," said Elizabeth.

"I asked him who was around the labs at night over the weekend. Jack covers Friday, Saturday, and Sunday nights. He said he walks through our buildings at the beginning of his shift, which is ten P.M., and then near the end of the shift. He doesn't keep an exact schedule, and he's supposed to vary his routine."

"The security guys check any lights they see," explained Louis. "So we get to know them if we're working late."

Elizabeth nodded.

"Jack remembers that on Friday Forrest Lang was around both at the beginning and end of his shift. He can't swear to exact times. He was in the lab itself the first time Jack saw him, and then upstairs at the photocopy machine the second time. Jack says that's not unusual; Forrest is around a lot at night."

"So I gather," said Elizabeth.

"Jack remembers Peter was in his office when he first stopped by Friday evening, but Peter was putting on his coat, and Jack saw him walk down the stairs like he was leaving the building."

"But he didn't see him go out?" asked Louis.

"No, it's not his job to follow professors to make sure they really are going home."

"OK, OK," said Louis.

"Then on Saturday, Jack said there were no lights on either time he came by. He just looks for lights from the outside, you see, and if there are none, and if the doors are locked up properly, he continues on his rounds. On Sunday night he had the stomach flu and called in sick. I asked if that meant there would be no one assigned to the science buildings, and he said that was right. They don't have substitutes, or whatever. The burglars are just supposed to stay home."

There was a pause. The clock in the Elliot living room ticked softly.

"It goes back to what I said to you, Mrs. Elliot,"

observed Louis. "We all could have done it, really. It's not as if there was a lack of opportunity. We all have keys to the doors, and we can avoid the security men easily by not turning on the lights. But none of us would have wanted Paul Chadwick dead, even though he was a jerk."

"He was more than a jerk," said Janet.

"OK, he was a sick guy. But because of his death, everybody in your lab lost letters of recommendation and all that goes with them. This murder has hurt everyone on your floor. And it doesn't help us third-floor people, either."

"But *someone* killed Paul Chadwick," replied Elizabeth. "We need a motive. Would you two think about what has been happening in the department, in terms of research, especially, since that seems the most important thing in your world?"

"It is," said Louis simply. Janet closed her eyes as if in thought.

"Could Chadwick have been in the process of borrowing somebody else's ideas again?" asked Elizabeth. "Plagiarism is a possibility in your field, I suppose, just like anywhere else. Could that get somebody ahead? If Paul Chadwick had found that one of you students was plagiarizing or cheating in some way, what would have happened?"

"The student would have been thrown out immediately," answered Louis without hesitation. "A student can't get away with the gray areas at all. But plagiarism, except for class work, isn't much of a possibility. In the journals we publish in, copied work would be recognized immediately. Maybe not in a thesis, but articles are carefully reviewed by outside people who are all specialists in the field."

Janet opened her eyes and said, "If something has been going on, it would have to be the theft of ideas. Or simply concocting data rather than making measurements."

"I'll look into what the fellows here have published recently and see if there are any irregularities. I think it's a long shot, though," said Louis.

"I would think so, too," answered Elizabeth, "except that someone killed Professor Chadwick." The Clerk pondered for a moment and then looked at Janet. "Did you order some timers and valves for your lab in the early part of the winter?"

"Yes, I did. From two different companies, I think. Anyway they came in two different packages, I remember."

"Did you use them?"

"No," said Janet. "I was going to rebuild part of the line this winter. So I ordered those parts and got some glass, too, from the chemistry stockroom here. But because of going to the deans, I never started."

"Do you know what would have happened to those things? The timers and such?"

"They should be on the top shelf above my bench. Way up high, next to the ceiling."

"Would you check and see if they're there? Let me know what you find."

The timer on the oven went off. The threesome adjourned to the kitchen.

Hoping to move them all toward a better subject to go with their meal, Elizabeth asked, "What do you hope to do when you leave Harvard?"

"I want to do a postdoc at MIT." He added in answer to Elizabeth's puzzled expression, "Post-doctoral studies are the normal stage after a Ph.D. in our subject. Postdocs are glorified grad students. MIT has the best program in our subject," he finished quickly.

"Do you have that lined up?" asked Janet. "They don't take on many postdocs in that department, you know."

"That's true. They've taken on Forrest Lang, though. At least that's what I heard yesterday. Apparently Peter moved heaven and earth and got him a spot in Judson's lab." Louis looked at Elizabeth and explained. "Judson's research group is the best in the world right now. It's a real honor to work there."

"Why on earth would they take on a slime like Forrest?" asked Janet.

"It's weird, isn't it? Peter must have said he could walk on water. But think of it this way: if Forrest got a place there, despite his stellar personality, how can they pass me up?"

Janet smiled. "Don't forget you'll be competing against me for an opening. I'll be done with my thesis by the fall."

Realizing that this subject was not suited to a peaceful meal, Janet turned the conversation by asking Elizabeth about her children and what they did. Answering her queries occupied the Quaker for some time. She was happy to speak about her boys.

When Elizabeth had awakened again to her responsibilities as hostess, Janet had finished eating, but she accepted a second glass of juice. After Louis had finished his third helping of chicken pot pie, Elizabeth offered the two students a ride to the Harvard campus. After collecting their coats, the three went off in the Quaker's car.

"Keep in touch," said Elizabeth as the graduate students climbed out of the old Chevrolet.

"Absolutely!" said Janet.

"God be with you both," said Elizabeth softly.

The two students crossed the law school grounds. Louis said he was going to stop in at the lab, and Janet decided to look for the timers and valves she had ordered. The pair crossed Oxford Street, and by the time they reached Divinity Avenue, they were walking hand in hand. Louis, delighted at the old familiarity they were recapturing, went with Janet up to Paul Chadwick's lab to prolong the time they were together. They saw no one on the stairs or in the hallways. The lab door was open, but no one was inside. Janet crossed over to her bench and looked at her things.

"I'm sorry I've been away from the work as long as I have. But now I'll make up for it." She opened the drawer under her bench and then looked more closely at the notebooks leaning against the wall at the back of her bench.

"Somebody's been in my notebooks," she said slowly.

"Really?"

"Uh, huh. I keep them in order by date. Goddamn it all!"

Louis peered at the spines of the notebooks, each of which had a date written on it.

"They look in order to me," he said, turning a questioning glance toward Janet.

"No, silly, I keep them in order right to left. The one I was using last should be here. Somebody's put them all backwards, left to right."

"I thought you said your bench was such a mess that Forrest complained to you about it!"

"All my samples are a mess. Scattered all over sometimes. But I care about the notebooks. My chemistry lab notebook won a prize in high school as the best in my class. I've stuck with that kind of record keeping."

"You impress me. My notebooks are covered with coffee stains," replied Louis. He looked around the lab thoughtfully. "Could somebody have been cleaning in here and rearranged things?"

"That would be a first!"

"Then somebody's been snooping."

"If somebody wanted to know what I was working up in the fall, I wish they'd ask, not just look through my stuff! What bastards!"

"There are some hard-nosed types around here." To divert Janet's anger he said, "Let's look at the oxygen line while we're both here. You're a lot more familiar with it than me. Have things been changed since you left in February?"

Janet was standing at the end of the line that gave the end product of the reaction.

"This is a new receptacle," she said, tapping a piece of glassware. "It makes sense. The old one was always a bit small. Eric or Forrest probably put that in recently." Slowly Janet walked down the line, looking at the snaking tubes and valves.

"This canister of chlorine pentafluoride is new since the murder, I suppose," she said with a grimace. "It would be the second one of the pair we ordered. The one that was on the line, the one that killed Chadwick, would have been emptied to fill the room. These valves on the line are all the same ones. Manual and greasy, like always. They've been here since I came. This manual valve at the start here is new. I suppose that's where the police found the electronic valve operated on a timer, do you think?"

"Yes, that's what Eric said to me. I know the police asked Eric and Forrest about it."

Janet walked back to her bench and climbed up on the counter. With her feet in her work space, she reached the highest shelf and took down two cardboard boxes. She handed them, one at a time, to Louis and then jumped back down to the floor.

"There's nothing here!" said Janet angrily as she looked through the packing materials in the two boxes. "Nothing at all! They not only read your notebooks around here, they also take your equipment when you're gone!"

Louis looked with concern into the boxes. He did not share Janet's anger; he felt only fear for her.

"This will look bad," he said softly. For the first time, Louis had some doubts about Janet's innocence.

He shook them off quickly as she said, "I don't give a Goddamn how it looks! But I care about what has been done with my stuff by the fucking men around here while I was gone. The cowards! They take advantage of you when you're down."

Still flushed with anger Janet climbed back up onto her bench and restored the boxes to their place. She climbed down more slowly than she had done a few minutes ago.

Louis looked at his watch and then paused awkwardly for a moment. "I've got to get to work. When can I see you again?"

"Breakfast," replied Janet promptly. "Let's meet at Dudley House like we used to in the fall."

"You're on," said Louis cheerfully, and they agreed on a time. After Louis went up to the third floor, Janet gathered up her lab notebooks, deciding to peruse them privately in her dormitory room. She wanted to remind herself of the work she had had in progress when her career was disrupted.

In her dorm room Janet carefully studied her notes. She was relieved to find they were complete and undamaged. The anger she had felt in the laboratory dissipated. As she looked at the work she had done just before running out of the building to the dean's office, she was glad to note that she had an interest in the data. She began to play with a new hypothesis in her mind that would explain one group of numbers. After some thought, as was her old custom, she wrote down the germ of her idea in her most recent notebook. Most such ideas did not work out, but it was worth recording them because they could lead to other thoughts.

Having finished that, Janet's mind returned to her troubles as a murder suspect. She decided to write a thank you note to Elizabeth Elliot for the meal she and Louis had just eaten. Mrs. Elliot, after all, had been a great help in recent days, and Janet's mother would be appalled if her daughter never sent a thank you in response to Elizabeth's hospitality. She was sure that writing a note would not occur to Louis. Men were not gifted when it came to certain forms of civility.

Janet was relieved to find a piece of decent stationery in her desk drawer. She thanked Elizabeth for her kindness and for the meal. She continued her note, explaining her discovery that her lab notebooks had been read during her absence from work. She mentioned that the oxygen line seemed normal, except for the end valve which the police had apparently taken away, but that the timers and valves she had ordered in the fall were missing from above her bench. Janet copied Elizabeth's street address from the Cambridge telephone book and stamped the envelope.

CHAPTER EIGHT

*We grope for the wall like the blind, and we grope as if
we had no eyes.*

ISAIAH 59:10

Janet called Elizabeth late on the following morning,
sounding discouraged.

"Today's mail had a letter from the administration
for me," said Janet in a flat voice. Elizabeth waited
for her to continue when she felt ready. "I guess it
shouldn't surprise me, but it does hurt my feelings,"
said Janet. She sniffed a bit. "Can I read it to you?"

"Of course."

"It's from Robert Williams. He's the Dean of the
graduate school. It's dated yesterday. 'Dear Janet,' it
says. 'I am writing to inform you that your complaint
against Professor Paul H. Chadwick is no longer considered active by the university. In light of Professor
Chadwick's death, no useful purpose can be served
by continuing our investigative process. We make no
finding in the case, but suspend it at this point.

" 'On a personal level, I would like to emphasize
that I admire your courage in bringing forward the

complaint. I know this matter has been painful for you. Best wishes, Robert Williams.' " Janet's voice was stretched thin and tight. "They make no finding! I've gone through all this grief for nothing? I wanted them to say that what happened to me in that lab was wrong! If they think that I'll go away quietly, they're denser than I thought!"

"The dean does say he admires your courage. I suspect that's a pretty rare statement from a dean."

"I don't give a damn what he admires! And he has no idea how much courage it takes to write a complaint like that; he has no conception!"

Elizabeth did not reply, deciding it was best simply to wait. Janet returned to the idea that the university should make a finding about her case and that she would accept nothing less. "They owe me a finding," she said as she was winding down from the tirade.

"I think they do, too," said Elizabeth. "But I'm afraid institutions are more cowardly than individuals. And Harvard has a lot to protect, by its lights."

"Why doesn't it think about protecting women students?" asked Janet in a bitter but more collected voice.

"You may have helped the university to think more about that," said Elizabeth. "Only time will tell. But you can be proud of what you did. It was the right thing, and not at all easy."

"I hope I can sue. But I think I should wait until I have my diploma in my hands."

"That sounds wise to me," answered the elder woman.

"Thanks. I get angry about these things. I appreciate your listening when I'm upset."

"That's OK. Being angry, I mean. And I'm sorry about the letter from the dean. But I suspect you have done a lot to educate the administration and your department." Elizabeth paused and then hazarded a hopeful statement. "Maybe by the time your daughters are grown up they will be welcome as equals at Harvard and Yale."

"I hope so. If they hurt my daughters like they've hurt me, I'll nuke this place till it glows in the daytime, if you'll excuse my saying so."

"Under the circumstances," replied the Quaker, "I will."

"But I plan on starting back to work in earnest today," said Janet. "I'll show those asses in my department that my work has been fine. Better than theirs!"

Later that morning, a phone call interrupted Elizabeth at her sewing machine as she was making a jumpsuit for her grandson Nicky. It was Joel Timmermann.

"I've had occasion to rethink some of what I said when we last talked," said Joel in professorial tones. "Perhaps I was rather hasty."

There was a silence. Elizabeth felt no need to break it.

"It may be that some women do run into difficulties at Harvard. Difficulties they're not responsible for, that is. I can see that, of course, and I never meant to say anything else."

Again Elizabeth waited silently.

With more strain in his voice Joel added, "I probably reacted a little too quickly, without listening to what you were saying about this student you met." He took a breath and added in a low tone, "I apologize for that."

"Thank you," said the Clerk warmly. "I think that a lack of listening was probably the root of the problem. I sat with the student and her distress was extreme."

"That's right," said Joel quickly. "I only heard about it secondhand. I didn't see her."

Elizabeth smiled. She did not actually begrudge Joel his need for an excuse, but she didn't feel it necessary to reassure him.

"The student newspaper and the *Boston Globe* are my only sources of information about the murder that's taken place in Janet's department," continued Joel. "We're all deeply grieved, of course, about what has happened there."

The Clerk was unsure to whom Joel's "we" referred. She answered by saying only, "I'm afraid the police have taken an interest in Janet simply because she is on record as complaining about Dr. Chadwick."

"I suppose she might have lashed out at him in a moment of rage," mused Joel.

"She did no such thing!" said Elizabeth impatiently. "And you do no one a service by spreading such speculation!"

"I haven't spoken to anyone at the university about this!" said Joel hotly. "I'm not a gossip!"

"I'm sorry if I implied that you were," said Elizabeth in a lower tone. "The murder was not done in a moment of rage or panic. It took some premeditation. At the time of Professor Chadwick's death, Janet Stevens was a long way from having the energy to plan anything."

"I'm sure you're right," said Joel in a noncommittal voice.

The Clerk closed the conversation as gracefully as she could by thanking Joel for taking the time to call. The two Quakers hung up on only slightly better terms than at the end of their last conversation.

At 3 P.M. on Friday afternoon Louis Lazier began to feel the need for coffee. He was doing a particularly tedious piece of lab work and was having trouble concentrating.

"Peter," he said across the lab, "I'm going down to the department office and snag a cup of coffee. Do you want one?"

"Great," the professor grunted. "I'll be here late tonight, and I'm already losing my edge."

As he climbed down the stairs to the department office, Louis thought about what he knew of Peter's work habits. Louis always went home by eight or nine o'clock. He worked six days a week, only taking time off for mass and TV-watching on Sundays. During his years in graduate school, working steadily, he had accumulated enough data for two good articles. If he had been more lucky in a few of his results, it would be three articles by now, but no more. Louis crossed the photocopy room to the coffeepot and carefully considered his advisor's work. Peter's articles were largely descriptive, packed full of measurements. He was not a man for calculations and model making. Louis paused at the coffeepot until a secretary's entrance into the room brought him out of his reverie. Slightly startled, he returned to the task at hand.

Carrying two paper cups of black coffee back into the lab, Louis crossed over to his advisor's side of the room.

"Here you go," he said. "A bad batch of java, as usual, but the price is right."

Peter smiled and thanked him. "How are things going?" he asked pleasantly.

"Slow. But OK. I'll be done with this counting today. Tomorrow I'll sit down at the Macintosh and start entering the data."

"Good!" said Peter. "Let me see it as soon as you have a plot."

"What are you working on?" asked Louis, sipping the bitter coffee.

"Finishing up my Archaen manuscript," answered Peter vaguely.

"Really!" exclaimed Louis. "You mean you've done all the mass spec runs already?"

"Yup. I've been here a lot of nights, I can tell you. The oxygen data are beautiful. And the carbon data are nearly a perfect fit to what I expected. I've already run it through the computer and got these plots out."

He pointed to a stack of papers under his elbow. He made no move, however, to show Louis the graphed data. There was no reason that he should, of course. Professors need not show their work to graduate students. Never in the past had Peter volunteered information to Louis about the work he did on his own. He was always very helpful about the student's work, and that was so rare at Harvard Louis had never thought beyond it.

Louis's thoughts as he drank his coffee were confused. He changed the subject by asking, "What did the National Science Foundation guy have to say to you at noon?"

"Good things! There's a real possibility of our getting some more funding for a new mass spec."

"That'll be nice," said Louis, slowly turning and walking back to his bench. He went back to his counting and struggled to keep his mind on his work.

Five minutes later Ruth Markham walked into the lab. She called out, "Peter, here's your article. Typed flawlessly; I proofed it."

"Great!" said Peter. "The figures are in my office. I'll go put the thing together." He raced from the room after Ruth handed him the manuscript.

The secretary looked around the lab with the eye of someone who distrusted the place. Seeing Louis she said abruptly, "So, another article out of the door for your advisor. You've not been getting much in print, have you? I thought you'd be writing your thesis by now!"

"I am writing, thank you," said Louis. "But I have a little more data to collect."

"Peter seems to get that done more quickly than you youngsters."

"Maybe he takes speed."

Ruth snorted and walked out of the room. Louis gave up counting and was soon lost in thought.

CHAPTER NINE

*Even them will I bring to my holy mountain, and make
them joyful in my house of prayer.*
ISAIAH 56:7

Palm Sunday did not go wholly unobserved even in
the secular atmosphere of Harvard Square. The multiple masses at St. Paul's provided the Square with
pulses of Catholics, just released from the Eucharist.
After escaping the dark interior of the old building,
they were happy for a stroll in the sun, walking
through the Square still holding their long palm
fronds. Children waved their palms and pushed them
in one another's faces. Adults carried theirs more
awkwardly, unsure what to do with this symbol of
triumphal entry. At noon, the cognoscenti of Harvard
Square, intent on worshiping in upwardly mobile
style, emerged from Christ Church, Episcopal. They
streamed into the flow of people. The Christ Church
contingent was carefully dressed. Some of the men
wore European suits, and the women all had on stylish
dresses. Episcopalian palm branches were of a tasteful
size, much smaller than the Catholic variety. Casually

attired Quakers moseyed quietly through the area all morning, going to and from their two Meetings for Worship. Without palms of any variety, they could be mistaken for part of the normal, secular background of Cambridge.

Louis Lazier held his large palm loosely as he left St. Paul's. The previous day he had gone to the paleontology library to use the library's computer search service. He had copied down the references for all the articles Peter had produced in the last seven years. Then he had gone to the stacks and found them. Photocopying them had taken an hour. He then carried them home, his heart heavy with what he might find.

In the evening he carefully read the articles, taking note of the quantities and types of data reported. He felt nauseous by the time he was through. When he woke on Sunday, he still felt sick. He was afraid of what he was thinking, afraid for Peter and for himself.

Louis had slept little and was deeply fatigued. He walked to St. Paul's for the late-morning mass, oblivious of the mild spring weather. The church was cold and dark. Louis knelt and began his Hail Marys as an old man genuflected in the aisle and took a place in the pew in front of him. The discipline of prayer, which took him back to his days in grade school, was a relief. Feeling more collected, he rose and sat down, waiting for the priest and the beginning of the service.

The organist began to play, the choir took its place, and the priest appeared. After a musical prelude, the liturgy began. The laity stood for the reading of the Gospel. The triumphal entry into Jerusalem, as described by Luke, was the passage for the day. According to the Scripture, if the people had not honored Jesus's entry to the city, the stones themselves would have cried out. The priest's homily on the Gospel was unmercifully long. He retold the entry scene and urged his listeners to look for Christ in this world, since His presence still needed celebration. From there the priest leapt into a discussion of the continuing importance of Lent in the modern world. The connection between this idea and the Gospel text was not clear to many listeners, but they waited patiently for the Eucharist, for which they had come.

Louis drifted away into his own thoughts. If Lent were meant to be a period for the faithful to set aside old habits, as he had been taught in school, then this was a good time to look at Peter Kolakowski's behavior in a new light. The problem was that Peter's fall would bring nothing but harm to his student's career. Scientific education, the last vestige of the apprenticeship system, had nothing but disadvantages if the master were not honorable. Louis had worked diligently in college, always hoping for a chance to do scientific research. His first year or two at Harvard had been demanding, and he often had considered leaving school and doing something easier. But he had persevered and now stood near his Ph.D. Two published articles, linking his name and work with the rising young Peter Kolakowski, would give him a chance at an exciting career. Although Louis knew all his own results were valid and his measurements real, he also now knew that anyone coming out of Peter's laboratory would be suspected of fraud. He might be able to redeem himself by further work, but it would be an uphill struggle. As the priest's voice rose and fell, saying something about Vatican II, Louis pulled his mind out of his troubles long enough to think about Janet. She, too, had invested her life in an education that was now backfiring. The priest summed up and led his listeners back to the spirit of Palm Sunday. Louis thought again of Peter. He could not be trusted in any way again.

The homily ended and everyone rose for a hymn. Louis stood and found his place in the hymnal. He no longer hesitated internally. Fraud in science was the same as mortal sin to the church. Louis returned his attention to the priest who was holding the host up and blessing it. When his turn came, he filed forward and received the Eucharist.

Elizabeth had heard the phone ringing as she came through her front door from Meeting for Worship. It had been Janet, who said she was in the Square and wished to come over. She had sounded agitated, saying that Louis had come to her dorm with some startling news about the department, and then asked if the two of them could come over to speak to her. Elizabeth then invited them for lunch and was now preparing a simple meal by reheating yesterday's soup and fixing ham sandwiches. It was not a proper Sunday dinner, but it would have to do.

The young people arrived, Louis still absentmindedly holding his palm. Janet looked at him with concern but smiled at Elizabeth. The Quaker invited them in, and Louis laid the palm on the coffee table. He sat down heavily on the sofa and shook his head.

"You don't look well," said Elizabeth. "How are you feeling?"

"Shaken," replied the youth. "I didn't sleep." He looked directly at her and continued in a low voice, "I've been telling Janet that I've checked out everything my advisor has published since he left graduate school. The output of data is phenomenal when you add it all up. In fact, it's impossible."

"Can you be sure of that?"

"I guess not sure the way you should be to swear to something in court. Maybe he did it all somehow, but I can't really believe it."

"I don't understand these things, of course, but is there some way you could be more certain?" asked Elizabeth.

"If we saw his lab notebooks, then we'd know," said Janet. "A good lab notebook is a careful record. You put in the details of what you do in lab each day, how the instrument you're using is behaving, what standards you used, and all that stuff."

"So if the data are real, Professor Kolakowski would have many such books?" asked the Quaker.

"Yes. And they should be in his office," said Louis. "In fact, I've seen them there. They're bound booklets, with hard covers. Two hundred pages long, each page numbered."

Elizabeth considered this.

"We can't ask to see them," said Janet, answering one of the Quaker's thoughts. "It's just not done. It would look like distrust."

"But you do distrust him," observed Elizabeth.

"Yes, but until I'm sure I'm right, I'm not going to let him know what I suspect. He holds my career in his hands," answered Louis.

"Could you look at them without his permission?" asked Elizabeth cautiously.

"If I broke into his office, I could," said Louis matter-of-factly.

"That seems wrong, of course, but I almost hope you will consider it," responded Elizabeth. She knew that what she was saying was most un-Quakerly. But, as usual when contemplating something to which her conscience objected, her stubborn and defensive feelings drowned out the better parts of herself. "I'm sure that something so unusual as cheating on this massive scale is tied up with the murder. It would be too freakish otherwise."

Elizabeth thought the soup must be hot. She invited the young people into the kitchen, where they sat down to lunch. She paused for a moment in silent prayer and then turned the conversation to Palm Sunday and how differently Catholics and Quakers observed the day.

"Your palm, Louis, reminds me what day it is, although we Friends don't observe the calendar in that way." Louis listened politely to Elizabeth's explanation that Quakers did not distinguish the different seasons of the year with religious observances. "The idea is easier than the practice of it, of course," said Elizabeth, "but we hope that each day is holy, as special to us as it is to God. And we fear we might lose that if we mark out some days with red letters."

"You don't decorate the Meetinghouse for different seasons the way the liturgical churches do," said Janet thoughtfully, "but you do treat Sunday like a red-letter day."

"That's true," replied the Clerk. "First-day is a bit special and we get together to observe it with worship. But there is scriptural authority for that."

"Not quite," said Louis in a friendly fashion. "Scripture says that God commands we rest and pray on the seventh day, not the first."

"You're right," answered Elizabeth easily. "I guess Friends are inconsistent when it suits our purposes."

"I don't say I'm particularly devout, and I sometimes miss mass, but things just wouldn't be the same to me without the rhythm of Advent, Epiphany, and Lent. To say nothing of Easter!"

"I think that's how my son Andrew feels about it. He's been an Episcopalian since his college days. It's all a little hard on me, as a Quaker mother. But I must admit he has found something that works for him. He tells me the liturgy is not so different from Quaker silence, once you get used to it."

"I don't know about that!" said Louis with a smile.

"Church services sure seem different from Quaker silence," said Janet. "Especially the smells-and-bells kind of churches. For myself, I like the simplicity of the Friends' approach."

"I've been to several church services during my life," said Elizabeth. "The thing above all others that seems foreign to me is the stained glass. That may seem strange to you, Louis, but when I sit in Meeting, in the silence, I can look out the windows because they're made of clear glass. I feel a part of the world around me, at unity with the trees and grass of Long-fellow Park. In the warm months we have the win-dows open and all of our spring Meetings are laced with birds' songs. Maybe that's why we feel no need for man-made music! I've seen some beautiful stained glass windows, but when you're inside a church, they certainly cut you off from the outside world."

"I think that's the idea," answered Louis. "The stained glass separates you from the mundane cares of daily living that you see outside. And the scenes the windows depict can inspire you to a different sort of consciousness, a higher state. It's not a question of being separated from nature, but being closer to spir-itual life."

The discussion continued in a friendly fashion as the meal was completed. The young people rose to go, and everyone's mind returned to the more stressful topic of Peter Kolakowski and his work.

As Louis put on his coat he said, "I'll think about how I can get into my advisor's office."

"I know I shouldn't encourage you to do so, but I wish you the best of luck," said Elizabeth soberly. She felt torn between her desire to see Janet in the clear and her concern not to promote deception or theft. She suppressed her conscience and smiled at the young man.

"Don't worry," he said lightly, "we Catholics can confess our sins. And we believe in extenuating circumstances. Besides, I'm a smart guy, and I won't get caught."

The Quaker shook her head in chagrin. She felt her stubbornness rising as she looked for ways of defending herself and Louis to the world. She knew Patience and other Friends would condemn her. For a moment she had an image of herself trying to explain the situation to her Meeting. It was a painful thought. Choosing the lesser of two evils was within Catholic, but not Quaker, tradition.

Louis's mind was settled, and he and Janet were ready to go. He thanked Elizabeth for the meal, took his coat, and departed with Janet. It was only after they were out the door that Elizabeth remembered the palm. She went into the living room where it lay, somewhat crumpled, on the coffee table. She held the palm in her hands, unsure what to do with it. After a moment's consideration, she put the frond in water. It seemed a shame to throw a green thing away, even if it might be an icon.

Elizabeth sat down at the kitchen table with her journal and began to bring it up to date. She recorded events without much difficulty but found it impossible to write down her confused feelings about what she had encouraged Louis to do. As she was nearing the end of her entry, the front doorbell rang.

Elizabeth's younger son stood on the front doorstep. She hugged him even before he had gotten fully inside. "So nice of you to stop by!" she said.

"There was a long vestry meeting after morning service, Mama, and then I went to lunch in the Square. Otherwise I'd have been here sooner," said Andrew. "I'm glad to see you looking well."

"I've been quite busy lately. It always does me good to feel needed," said Elizabeth. "Tomorrow I'll be trying something new. I'd like to talk to you about it."

Andrew sat down in the living room, and his mother described to him the letter she had received from his old childhood friend John Anderson, and Ralph Park's knowledge of him through prison visitation work. She explained that John would stay with her immediately after his release from Concord the following day.

"But, Mama! This is crazy! Anderson's been in prison for rape! You can't have him here! I forbid it!"

"I'm not sure that you can," said Elizabeth quietly.

"I guess I can understand your meeting with him, if you want, but don't take a felon into our house here!"

"It's still my house," said Elizabeth more sharply, "and I do what I feel led to do."

Andrew was silent for a moment, wondering how he could argue against a Quaker who felt "led."

"I'm sorry if I spoke harshly, and I have no right to forbid anything," he began. "John and I used to play basketball and I remember those days fondly. I'm sure there is something good in him. But he's spent at least several years incarcerated on that charge. Maybe it was statutory rape, I'm not sure, but you know what the state prison system is like. He's been living with brutal men for years." Andrew concluded by shaking his head as he said, "Have you stopped for a moment to consider your own safety?"

"I think I understand how serious prison experience is. But I remember him when you two were in junior high and used to play together. It seems clear to me that I could try to give him a new chance when he gets out. I have no one here to inconvenience. But apart from all that, I feel called to this, Andrew. It is a witness."

Her son sighed. His quick temper was exceeded only by his mother's stubbornness. He knew it was pointless to argue, and he changed the subject to family matters. He told his mother of his promotion at his engineering firm and inquired after his older brother, Mark. Elizabeth listened and chatted until it was clear he was ready to go.

"Hey," said Andrew as he rose from the sofa, "you have a palm on the mantel? I'd almost think you went to church today!"

"No, no," said Elizabeth hastily. "I was at Meeting. But a friend of mine stopped by, and he left that here accidentally." Fearing her son's disapproval, she did not want to explain in what she was involved at Harvard.

Andrew considered what she had said. "I hope he's

a nice fellow," he said softly. "And of course I'm glad he's a churchman."

"Oh, Andrew! It's not like that at all. He's just a kid, and he came here with his girlfriend. Or someone soon to be his girlfriend, by the looks of things."

"I'm glad you're not in any danger from that quarter," said Andrew more cheerfully. "It's been good to talk, but I must be getting home. I assume Mark and his wife will invite us all over for Easter like last year. See you soon!" He kissed his mother, left the house, and walked up Concord Avenue in the direction of Upland Road, where he had a small apartment.

Elizabeth treated herself to a cup of tea after Andrew had left and returned to the living room with her Earl Grey. Glancing out her window, she looked idly at the passersby on Concord Avenue. Most were now carrying the coats that had been necessary in the morning. The sun continued strong, and the scene on Concord Avenue had the definite look of spring. In Elizabeth's long experience, students became abundant not only in the Square and near the Charles, but everywhere in Cambridge as soon as the weather turned springlike. The warmth and sun, however transitory, combined with the natural urge to avoid study, sent pairs and trios of students wandering all over Cambridge.

This afternoon was no exception. Two students were just entering Elizabeth's field of view from the direction of Harvard. Looking at a striking black woman and a twiggy Caucasian walking on her sidewalk, the Quaker speculated that they were off for a walk around Fresh Pond. That walk was a favorite even of older women, at least those who, like Elizabeth, could still do two or three miles at a stretch. Perhaps if this weather held, she could tour Fresh Pond on the morrow.

Watching the pair reminded Elizabeth of some of her own spring afternoons as a student more than forty years ago when she and Rebecca Nichols had shared a tiny dormitory room at Wellesley College, upriver from Boston. Elizabeth remembered her delight with the Charles and its changing moods in the spring. Her roommate, who had grown up in Washington State, disparaged New England. She thought it quite unremarkable. But to a Yankee like Elizabeth, even the simple beauties of tulips coming into bloom or the sun warming the maples into bud were enough to make memories of Massachusetts ice storms recede into nonreality.

The two students on Concord Avenue had disappeared when Elizabeth came out of her musing and again faced the reality of what she was condoning in Louis's plans and what she feared about John Anderson. She thought again of her promise to Neil and to herself to catch him up on the events of her life. She called him, but there was no answer at his house.

It was 2 A.M. as Louis walked through Harvard Square. Three cabs were at the taxi stand in front of an all-night coffee shop and several undergraduates were walking along Massachusetts Avenue. He stepped onto Harvard's property and cut across the Yard toward Oxford Street and Divinity Avenue.

The main doors of the paleontology building were double-locked, but his key opened them without difficulty. Louis walked up the stairs to the third floor. Both the stairway and hallway were lit dimly by safety lights. A small flashlight in Louis's hand assisted him.

Peter Kolakowski's office was at the end of the hallway, directly above Ruth Markham's on the second floor.

Louis tried his key in the lock of Peter's door. The door had a frosted glass panel, and he tried to peer into the office for a moment. As he had anticipated, the lock did not respond. He examined the wooden frame around the door. In an old building like this one, the wood was painted into place. If he removed any of the molding, the damage would be obvious in the morning.

His hand felt the far side of the doorframe. He stopped suddenly and smiled. The hinge was on this side of the door! At some point this old building had been remodeled, and it had seemed sensible to someone for the door to open outward into the hall.

Louis found a screwdriver and a hammer in the laboratory. Working slowly and making as little noise as he could, he removed the pins from the hinges. Hoisting the oak and glass door sideways required all his strength.

Half an hour later he fully understood his advisor's

transgressions. He held in his hands all of Peter's laboratory notebooks. There were only four. The first contained the research that Louis recognized as Peter's dissertation project when he was earning his Ph.D. The second notebook contained records of two projects, the first of which involved data on a rare fossil species. It was a project Louis had never seen. He was sure Peter had never published it. Not publishing the results seemed reasonable: even in the narrow beam of a small flashlight, it was obvious that the data were hopelessly scattered. Variables other than the ones of which Peter had been cognizant must have been important.

The second half of the notebook contained the beginning of a project on Paleozoic trilobites, a subject that Louis recognized from the published record. To his amazement, the data in the notebook were few and highly variable. Louis's memory of the article on the trilobites was clear. Peter had published reams of measurements about the size and changing proportions of different trilobite species over time. All of the published data were similar and showed the same trend.

Louis checked the date of the second notebook. It corresponded to the year in which Peter had published on this problem. The third and fourth notebooks were blank. They were the same style and size as the first two, clearly purchased at the same time for similar use. But nothing had been recorded in them.

Quickly putting away the laboratory notebooks, Louis sat down at Peter's personal computer and turned it on. He searched the hard disk for data files. Calling them up to the screen, he looked at long columns of isotopic and other measurements. Louis knew that if these data were real, they would have been recorded on paper in the lab before being typed into the computer. He continued to move through the hard disk. By chance he noticed a similarity in the data he had on the screen to a data set he had called up before. The first column on the screen had begun:

   2,3,5,7,11 . . .

and the sequence had stuck in Louis's mind because the values were a list of prime numbers. Checking the earlier record, he found that the columns of numbers were identical in both data sets.

Louis shut down the computer, put the door back on its hinges, and walked back to his apartment. When he got there, he checked his Xeroxed articles just to be sure. The two identical data sets he had found in the computer were published in two articles under Peter's name on different topics. The raw data values had been used in conjunction with completely different organisms.

CHAPTER TEN

He shall not fail nor be discouraged, till he have set judgment in the earth.
ISAIAH 42:4

Ralph Park stopped his car in front of Elizabeth's house. She swung her coat around her shoulders and hurried outside. It was raining heavily this Monday morning, and the Clerk held her umbrella over her head until she gained the safety of the car.

"Good morning, Friend!" said Ralph. "It's wet. But any day is a good day to get out of prison."

"Do you know the way to Concord prison?" asked Elizabeth in a flutter. "I just realized I've not been over in that direction for a great many years."

"Yes," answered Ralph. "Most of the prison visitation I do is at Norfolk, but I've been to Concord, too." Before he pulled away from the curb he asked, "Did you bring your letter from Meeting explaining your status as a minister?"

"The letter is in my purse," answered Elizabeth with more calm. "It's signed by myself, of course, as

Clerk, which seems a bit strange. But I had Harriet countersign it as Meeting secretary."

"That'll be all right," said Ralph as he entered traffic. The cars passing in the opposite direction sprayed Ralph's old and rusty Citation with water. "The guards just need something on letterhead stationery that looks official. I don't think we'll have to submit to strip searches when we go inside. But if they do tell us we're not ministers, we can put on nun's habits; I've got a couple in the trunk."

Elizabeth smiled but could not enter into the joke. She still felt uncomfortable with the palm in her living room.

"Just being a plain minister will have to do," she said quietly.

"I take it you were satisfied with John Anderson when you spoke to him on the phone?"

"Oh, yes. He called and we had a long talk. He said he was on the same basketball team as Andrew in school, and I remember that. He remembers coming to our house when the boys were in junior high."

"It's been a long stretch for him inside. It's hard to know what makes it possible for some of the guys to get a new start."

"He wants me to believe he's headed for new things. That much is clear." Elizabeth paused, then added thoughtfully, "Who can say what's in his heart? He was convicted of second-degree sexual assault, by the way, not statutory rape. As he described it, it was what they call a date-rape situation. A woman he had gone out with for a long time, whom he was 'on social terms with,' you might say, decided one evening she didn't want what he did. He says she often said 'no' when she meant 'yes.' Men always say that, of course, but I suppose a few women give them cause to believe what they want. Then he violated parole when he got out of the minimum security place he'd been sent, and resisted arrest when they came to take him back. He was sent back to Concord. Anyway, he says he has every desire to stay out of prison, and that seems genuine."

"Repeat felons want to stay out, too," said Ralph cautiously. "But maybe this is a situation where a new start might be possible."

The trip to Concord went quickly, principally due to Ralph's expert and aggressive driving. Elizabeth was relieved when the car stopped in the prison's parking lot. They got out into the fine rain that was now falling and hurried to the main doors. A prison guard spoke briefly to Ralph, ignored Elizabeth's letter, took them down a hallway, and left them in a small room. Many minutes passed. Ralph smoked a cigarette and then another. In Elizabeth's youth, Quakers never smoked, but she refrained from commenting. Eldering younger Friends was something Elizabeth preferred to leave to Quakers like Patience. Time passed slowly.

"From the work I've done in the prison system over the years, I can tell you there's a lot of waiting around in these places. It's the routine," observed Ralph. "The prisoners and guards spend half their day waiting."

"That can't be easy," said Elizabeth.

Silence returned. Elizabeth took the opportunity to pray, and a few more minutes passed.

"Here he is," said the guard, swinging open the door and motioning for the Quakers to come out into the hallway.

A young man with dirty blond hair and blue eyes stood in the hallway.

"I'm Ralph Park."

"And you must be Mrs. Elliot," said John Anderson, turning toward the elder Quaker. "You haven't changed a bit."

As soon as Elizabeth and John entered the house on Concord Avenue, he launched into conversation.

"I know it's not easy to invite someone like me into your house," he began. "Nothing about this is easy for me, either. Second-degree sexual assault is like being branded. It's tough for me to be anything but a god-awful rapist in the eyes of almost everybody. I bet Andy isn't happy about your having me here."

"No," said the Quaker honestly, "he isn't."

"I'm not surprised. But I'd like to explain that they convicted me of a rape charge on the word of my old girlfriend. It was what she said versus what I said. I admit I'm not a saint. I wasn't then, and I'm not now. But that woman didn't tell the truth. And the judge was a woman, which didn't help. Not that a lady couldn't be fair, but just that that one wasn't."

"I didn't know the Commonwealth had any women judges," said Elizabeth.

"There's one, at least, and I got her. She ruled against everything my lawyer said, right from the start. It all depends on who you choose to believe, you see. Debbie said she hadn't led me on at all that night, which was insane. And she claimed she said 'no,' but I was there and I didn't hear it. There was no clear 'no,' nothing you could believe she meant. Some women tease a lot, and she was one of that sort. Not that the judge thought about that much, I'm sure."

"You felt the judge wouldn't listen to your side of the story?"

"No way. She looked at me like I was a square egg. She was totally biased, right from the start. It was a foregone conclusion I'd be convicted. Then, when I got out, I admit I was pretty crazy, and I did some stupid things. I didn't go to my meetings with the parole guy. I got pulled over for a moving violation and ended up in a fistfight with the cop. So I was sent to Concord to do the rest of my time for what Debbie did to me. And then more for resisting arrest and stuff. Being in prison for any reason is hell, but I was branded a rapist by the system, you see, and that's the worst thing you can be inside. The murderers and the guys in for armed robbery take everything out on you. All because of what one woman said about one night!"

The ringing telephone interrupted the conversation, saving Elizabeth from having to think of a reply.

"I'm sorry to disturb you again, Mrs. Elliot," began Janet over the telephone. "But I wanted you to know what's happened. Detective Burnham sent two cops here to my dorm this afternoon, and they took me down to his office. I called Mr. Gibson, and he came down, too."

"Good," said Elizabeth. "Was he helpful?"

"I don't know," said Janet. "Some questions he let me answer, and some he didn't. I can't tell what sense it makes, having a lawyer. He was right about one thing, though, when we spoke to him in his office. They wanted my fingerprints. I still have ink all over my hands."

"The ink is nothing to be ashamed of. During World War II my older brother was in prison for refusing the draft. The government probably still has a record of his fingerprints somewhere, but the ink washed off long ago."

"Thanks."

"What did Mr. Burnham ask you about?"

"About my complaint against Chadwick and when it was I'd last talked to him. About the valves in the oxygen line. And a lot of questions about timers."

"Does he know that you had ordered some timers and valves earlier in the year?"

"Yes! He asked me about that and what I'd done with them. Mr. Gibson told me not to answer. He was startled, I think, because we hadn't had a chance to discuss it."

"What else was on the detective's mind?"

"He wanted to know how many canisters of chlorine pentafluoride we had in lab and where they were kept. Who would know about them, and stuff like that. I tried to explain that everything toxic in a lab is clearly labeled. Anybody can see what's chlorine pentafluoride and what isn't. Just now I've been afraid you'll lose faith in me. If you and Mr. Gibson believe I'm guilty, I don't know where I'll turn."

"I'll never believe you guilty of anything in this matter but bad luck. And Mr. Gibson's beliefs are not relevant one way or another. He's a lawyer, and lawyers work on behalf of their clients no matter what their own feelings. I do think the questions about the canisters may be important. How many of them have been in the lab this year?"

"Well, there was the one we were using in the fall. When it started to get low, we ordered two more. We don't use much of the gas, but there can be a problem getting a supply. There's only one chemical company left that makes it on a commercial basis. It's highly toxic, and demand for it must be pretty low. So we order two at a time when we can get it."

"Did the two new canisters arrive promptly in the fall?"

"Yes. I remember I was there when they were delivered. I signed for them. They came just as the old canister was hitting rock bottom. We replaced it with one of the new ones that same week, I think."

"What happens to the used canisters?"

"They're disposed of like toxic waste. In case there's a trace of chlorine pentafluoride in them, you see. Somebody from lab calls Harvard's toxic waste men. You just fill out a form, because they charge the lab for the service, and one of them comes by and picks it up. In our building, we just leave things on the loading dock for those guys with the signed form taped on the canister. It saves them having to come upstairs."

"What's become of the second canister, do you know?"

"That's the one that's on the line now. The police took the other one away, but it would have been empty except possibly for traces of gas." Janet sighed. She seemed to be at the end of what she had to say. Elizabeth explained she had a houseguest and needed to show him his room, and the two women said good-bye.

The Quaker looked at John, who had seated himself at the kitchen table during the telephone conversation. He was taking a package of cigarettes from his shirt pocket. Elizabeth was startled but recovered quickly.

"John, if you smoke here, I'd appreciate your doing it outside."

Equally startled, John jammed the packet back into his pocket and mumbled that he could wait for a while before he needed one.

"Come upstairs," said the Quaker. "You can unpack. I'll put you in Andy's old room." Elizabeth slowly climbed the steps to the second floor. "It seems appropriate, and Mark's old room was long ago converted into a sewing room for me."

John, carrying his duffel bag, followed behind her.

He looked into the room she indicated and said, "Thanks. This is fine."

"The bathroom is just down the hall," she said, indicating with her hand the direction of her own room as well.

He put down his bag and looked out the dormer window of the small room. The view was toward Concord Avenue.

"It's nice to see a street with people walking by," he said.

"Good."

A young, smartly dressed woman was passing in front of the house.

"That's the kind of woman that gets you in trouble," said John pointing toward her. "A good-looker, and knows her way around. You can't trust what she'll say about you."

Startled again, Elizabeth did not know how to reply. John interpreted her pause as encouragement to continue.

"I can't help but think of my old girl when I see any good-looking broads. But they're all the same— dangerous, really, if you think about it."

"I hope that's a bit of an exaggeration. We're not in a conspiracy against you men."

"Not ones like you, of course. But look at that woman that testified against the Supreme Court guy! It was all about something that supposedly happened ten years before! How could she have remembered what she said she did?"

"I'd guess that it was seared into her mind," said

Elizabeth quietly. She, too, had watched the hearings.

John shook his head derisively. "Well those days are seared into his, now. But the authorities believed the man, for a change."

Elizabeth was suddenly uncomfortable pursuing such a topic with John in a small bedroom. She said she would be downstairs and left him to unpack.

At breakfast the following day Elizabeth asked John if he wanted one egg or two.

"Two please. It's nice to have real eggs. I worked in the prison kitchen for two years. We did eggs at breakfast sometimes, but it was always powdered eggs. We mixed it with milk. The milk was from powder, too. It was supposed to be like scrambled eggs, but it wasn't great."

"I remember powdered milk and powdered eggs during the thirties," replied the Clerk. "Maybe during the war, too, when I think about it."

"You sound like my parents. They always talk about the thirties and forties."

"Is your mother still here in Cambridge?"

"No, my real mother's been dead a long time. Which is maybe just as well, seeing how things turned out with me the last few years."

Elizabeth did not know how to reply.

"Nobody can be proud when their boy goes to prison," continued John. "Although in lots of ways the guys inside aren't really all that bad. Trouble is, they just don't give a shit. Not about other people and sometimes not even about themselves. I was glad when you Quakers did that project at Concord. I didn't know Andy Elliot's mother was a Quaker, or I would have asked after you." He accepted a plate of two sunnyside-up eggs.

Elizabeth sat down at the table to tea and toast. She prayed silently for a moment, then began to eat. John had a mouth full of eggs when he noticed that Elizabeth was praying. He did his best to be silent and still until she was finished.

"Mostly the only religious people in prisons are the Fundamentalists," continued John. "Trying to save your soul. You're in danger of hellfire! That kind of thing. But you know, in that Concord project, none of the Quakers preached at us. That's what got my respect, I guess. I asked Ralph why Quakers don't preach. He said he figured everybody's soul was already saved."

"That's what a lot of Quakers in this Meeting would say," replied Elizabeth. "We really don't have thought-out ideas on questions like salvation."

"Why not?"

"Just trying to live right seems to keep most Quakers busy. If we serve God in our daily lives and our work, that's enough."

"Does that mean you take cons into your house to serve God?"

"I felt called to make contact with you. I remember you. That's enough. Enough for me, and I hope for you."

"Sure," replied John. "I was just wondering." He rose from his chair. "I'm going over to Boston this morning to see a friend of mine."

"Fine. If you're back by six o'clock, there'll be supper here for you," said Elizabeth.

After John left, Elizabeth went out into the gusty morning to replenish the bird feeders. The juncos and a pair of cardinals that frequented Elliot property appeared quickly when she returned into the house. Elizabeth considered their presence a blessing. She made herself a little more tea and watched them for a moment from the window. The phone disturbed her meditations. It was Janet.

"Louis has come up with something. And I'm glad to say he didn't get himself arrested at the same time."

"Thank the Lord," said Elizabeth reverently.

"He found what we suspected, I'm afraid. It really shakes your faith in everything you've worked for. I wanted you to hear of this right away—that's why I called. Let me put him on the line and he can give you the details."

The phone was transferred to the young man.

"Hi, Mrs. Elliot. I let myself into Peter's office last night, and I've looked at his lab notebooks. They're pathetic. He's really only done two projects since coming to Harvard. They were pretty small in scale and they didn't work out! The notebooks are clear enough about that. I'm sure now he's been publishing data he's made up." Louis sighed. Elizabeth waited patiently for him to continue.

"Not only is he a liar, he's been stupid about it! I

found a duplicated set of numbers in two data sets in two different articles. They're about completely different things. He just copied a set of numbers in his computer and renamed the variables he was claiming he had measured."

"I'm so sorry," said Elizabeth sadly.

"There's no need to apologize!"

"I'm not apologizing," said the Quaker, "only expressing sorrow."

The student regained his footing. "I'm sorry, too," he said, "because it means my career is screwed. I'm Peter's student. We've published together! When I expose him, all my work and my results will be called into question. And what is a letter of recommendation from Peter going to be worth when this comes out? There's no choice but to tell our colleagues what a fraud he is, but when I do I'll suffer almost as much as he does."

"Do you think anyone else in your department knows about Peter's dishonesty?"

"No. They'd speak up if they knew. A lot of them would be glad to tear Peter apart. Men like Professor Scott, our chairman, would be glad to destroy somebody for this sort of thing. Publicly they'd wring their hands and say they felt compelled to do the right thing, but in private they'd be glad. Peter has been soaking up an awful lot of grant money, and with him out of the way there'll be more for others.

"But I hope I don't feel too sorry for myself," said Louis reverting to his earlier subject. "My career is in no worse shape than Janet's, really. And she certainly didn't do anything wrong. She's got no letter of recommendation, either, and nobody will want to have a 'troublemaker' like her in their lab any more than they'd want a 'fraud' like me. There, that got a smile out of Janet, at least."

"I'm glad you two are together. I hope the situation isn't as bad as it looks to you now," responded Elizabeth. "It may be that the other professors in your department could review your work and see that it is separate from your advisor's. If your notebooks are in order, I suspect that something can be done. Especially if you come forward with this information about Professor Kolakowski."

"We'll see," said Louis. "Anyway, Janet wanted to let you know what I'd found."

"Thanks to both of you. And what you said, plus some other things, have given me an idea that could clear all this up. At least I think so. Could I get your help once more? No more breaking and entering, you understand," said the Quaker to reassure Louis and quiet her own conscience. "But perhaps the smallest amount of deception. And a project about checking references in a student's piece of scientific work."

Louis listened to what was asked of him and agreed to the tasks.

"I'd be glad to do both those things."

Elizabeth thanked Louis for calling.

Elizabeth's doorbell summoned her to the front of her house just after five o'clock. Ruth Markham stood on

her step, and the Clerk invited her into the living room
and offered to make tea.

"No thanks. I don't need entertaining. I just got off
work and was walking to the subway. I'm sorry I
missed the Business Meeting the other night. I wanted
to come but it didn't work out because of Timmy's
homework schedule. He had a lot to accomplish that
night, and his father can't be trusted to oversee his
homework. It just doesn't get done."

Elizabeth said that she understood.

"But I'm interested in the handicap-access question
before Meeting. My mother is wheelchair bound, so
it strikes home. What do you think of this proposal
to put in a ramp, but hide it all around the back so as
not to spoil the view of our quaint building? I know
you'll say I'm cynical, but isn't the real reason some
Friends want to keep it all in the back parking lot just
vanity? It's farther for the wheelchairs and the old
people to get to if they come from the street!" The
boisterous Friend continued without pausing for
breath. "We should have put in a ramp when I was a
kid. We've postponed it for a generation because of
not wanting to spend the money. And now we're talking about putting a ramp in, as long as we don't have
to look at it."

"It's not quite as bad as all that," said Elizabeth.
"A ramp in the back does make sense if you think
about those Friends who use the tiny parking lot."

"Only five percent of us can use that lot!" said Ruth
hotly. "It's just a sophist argument to put the thing
out of sight. You know how absurdly proud Hugo is

of Quaker tradition and Quaker history. And he's
stuck on a certain image of Friends. Mixed in with a
lot of old New England money, of course, and private
schools and all the rest."

"Hugo can be a little parochial at times, but I've
noticed that in several Friends, myself included. We
shouldn't be too quick to judge, lest we ourselves be
judged."

"Hah! I can stand up to Hugo Coleman's judgment
any day."

Elizabeth knew from long experience that Ruth was
not as upset as she sounded. It was just her style of
conversation. Ruth was an atypical Friend.

"I'm sure you won't let Meeting be bamboozled by
a few old Friends who fancy themselves too much,"
said Ruth.

"I doubt Meeting can be railroaded into anything.
The Spirit won't abandon us so completely." Elizabeth paused and looked intently at Ruth. "On another
subject, Friend, I was hoping for some help from
you."

"What's that?"

"You have keys that open the professors' offices in
your department, don't you?"

"Yes, I've got the mother of all master keys. All
the secretaries do. Why?"

"Have the police blocked off Paul Chadwick's office?"

"They did at first. But they took down their tape a
while ago. What do you have in mind?"

"I'd like to look around his office. I'm not entirely

sure what I hope to find, but it's related to some things the police don't know about. Louis Lazier and I think there's been at least one other mystery in your department besides this murder. I'm sure the two are connected."

"Are you going to make yourself any clearer than that?"

"Not for the present, if you'll forgive me. Louis and perhaps some others are affected, through no fault of their own. It's best to wait. Can you trust me? I just want to look around. I give you my word I won't take anything."

"I predict you won't find anything but the usual academic junk, but sure, come back with me now. I'll let you in and stay with you. That way, if somebody comes—and I don't imagine anyone will—I'll just say I was looking for purchase order forms that were being processed when Paul Chadwick was killed. I really do need to look through his desk and mail for that sort of thing. We have to close down his grants now, and that means bringing all the accounting up to the present."

"Excellent." Elizabeth fetched her navy blue coat and hat, and the two women walked down Concord Avenue. It was sunset, and the air was growing cooler.

"We'll have a snowstorm on Easter," said Ruth with characteristic optimism.

Elizabeth smiled. The two women reached the paleontology building on Divinity Avenue. Leaving the sunset behind with a sigh, Elizabeth entered the world of artificial light on Ruth's heels. Climbing up to the second floor, the secretary unlocked her office door and hung up her coat.

"There's another thing, Friend," said Elizabeth. "Can you tell me how many canisters of chlorine pentafluoride were disposed of by the toxic waste people in the fall and also this winter?"

"Yes. There's a form for that, because the lab gets charged. Harvard is too cheap to foot the bill."

She motioned for Elizabeth to sit down as she opened a filing cabinet. In a moment she pulled out two papers.

"There was one taken away in November. The police took away the one that was on the oxygen line when we found Chadwick. It was nearly empty, Eric told me. He told Burnham they shouldn't just put it in police storage because it's so dangerous. Burnham didn't pay any attention to him.

"But let's get a move on," said Ruth. She stood up and walked down the hall with Elizabeth close behind. She unlocked Paul Chadwick's office door and switched on the lights. Elizabeth entered the small, cell-like room and looked around as Ruth shut the door. Books and journals were arrayed on shelves on all the walls. The small space had only one window and was cramped and unpleasant.

"Not a cheery place to work," said Elizabeth.

"He wasn't a cheerful man. This office is so small, he used to meet with people in the lab. They'd have room to spread out papers on the counters there. He used this just as a place to write and to store his books and records."

Elizabeth looked at the nearest shelves. She ran a finger along the edge of one and made a face.

"That's the police dust. They sprayed a lot here and in the lab, looking for fingerprints. The students cleaned up the lab as soon as they were let in. It's not exactly the best condition for their work, having dust all around. But nothing has been cleaned up in here."

Elizabeth looked around the shelves with care. They were full of books and journals. There were some looseleaf notebooks on one shelf and, in one corner, bound notebooks. Elizabeth squatted on the floor and withdrew one of the bound notebooks. Each page was completely filled with a tiny script. The entire notebook was used to capacity. The dates on the pages were all from the spring of 1959. Looking at the other notebooks, she found dates scattered throughout the sixties.

Ruth had been looking over Elizabeth's shoulder. "He did a lot of analytic work in the lab when he was young, I guess. But it's not normal for professors to keep that up once they get tenure. They're too busy writing grants, advising students, and putting books together."

Elizabeth stood up stiffly. The arthritis in her knees made her wince. She glanced quickly at the few shelves she had not studied.

She sat down at the desk and began to look at the dust-covered papers that were piled high on its top. She sneezed. She shifted two stacks of paper covered with writing in a tight, cramped hand.

"Those two piles are Paul's manuscript for a book

he was working on. He wrote the first draft by hand. I put it on the word processor from there," explained Ruth. "This stack is his copy of the article he and Eric have been doing. I recognize the title."

"Look at all these Xeroxes. Do they mean anything to you?" asked Elizabeth.

"No. I didn't copy them for him. That's strange, really."

Elizabeth took the stack of copies onto her lap. The titles were complex and might as well have been written in Urdu. But the author's name was Peter Kolakowski. She turned to the second article and saw that it, too, had Peter as the sole author. The third and fourth articles were the same. The fifth article had two other names following Peter's.

"Who are these people?"

"That first name is a technician we used to have working here. Not a bad guy, but he didn't stay long. He left five years ago. The second name I don't recognize at all."

Ruth took the article from Elizabeth's hand and perused it more closely. "It's strange that the publication date is so recent. That technician has been gone a long time. And the address listed for the third author is this department, which can't be right. I've never heard of P. D. Richardson in my life. I didn't type this; Peter never gave it to me. He must have done it on his computer."

The last three articles had only Peter's name as author. A legal pad was under the final article. And below that was a hard-bound copy of something by

Eric Townsend. Looking at the title page, Elizabeth saw it was Eric's senior thesis submitted to Princeton. On the legal pad, the same small, cramped handwriting had listed the articles by Peter Kolakowski by publication year. Next to the articles' titles was a column labeled "data reported." Entries included such items as "112 oxygen isotope analyses." Other types of analyses which Elizabeth could not understand were also totaled up. There was no reference to Eric Townsend's work.

"What do you make of this?" asked Elizabeth, handing the legal pad to Ruth.

"It's Paul's writing for sure. I guess he was taking an interest in Peter's work. Checking it all out. I know Peter's reputation has really grown in the past several years. He was something of a threat to Chadwick."

"Why didn't the police take these papers, I wonder?" said Elizabeth softly.

"Maybe it looked like routine work to them. Professors do read a lot of journal articles, you know. It's the normal thing. They were here only one day. That first subway killing pulled the big detective off onto those murders."

"Our tax dollars don't seem to buy careful police work these days," mused Elizabeth.

"Not that they ever did!" retorted Ruth.

Elizabeth said nothing but returned the legal pad and the stack of photocopies to the desktop. She opened the top desk drawer and looked at the clutter of ballpoint pens, paper clips, and Post-it Notes. In the second desk drawer she found nothing more exciting. "I wonder if he had an appointment book," she mused.

"Certainly. One of those big, pretentious ones from *The New Yorker* or *The Wall Street Journal* or something. But that was one of the things the police took away."

Elizabeth looked idly back into the first drawer, unsure whether she should stay any longer but not yet ready to go. She took out the larger of the two Post-it Notes pads.

"We didn't have these when I was young," said Elizabeth.

"They're quite new, and awfully convenient. Like Scotch tape, you wonder how the world ever got along before Post-it Notes were invented."

As Elizabeth tipped the pad in her hand and began to return it to the drawer, the fluorescent light above her struck the surface of the top note at an angle. She saw indentations. Turning the pad slowly at various angles she saw tiny shadows along the lines that had been impressed into the paper.

"I might be able to read this," said Elizabeth slowly, putting her nose down to her work. "Like in *North by Northwest*."

"The old film? Read what?" asked Ruth.

"Whatever Mr. Chadwick wrote on his last note."

"It probably just says 'Ruth: I need this typed by Tuesday.' "

Elizabeth peered at the note for a long time. She shook her head. "The first word is 'Peter.' It's much darker—or I should say deeper—than the rest. It's underlined. It goes on: 'This is a list of something-something-something and I want to something-something-something.' But I can't make out the lighter letters."

"I don't see what this can tell you, but let me look." Ruth squinted at the paper. "It's too faint. And his writing was so small, anyway, it was tough to read even with ink on the paper."

"I want to keep this, Ruth."

"Now you're stealing Harvard property, Friend!" said Ruth with a smile. "But I've taken a few Post-it Notes home myself."

"Don't tease me like that. It's only the top one I want." She tore it off carefully and returned the notes to the drawer.

Elizabeth rose from the desk chair. She straightened out the papers on the desk to return them to the places they had originally been, then followed Ruth out into the hall. Elizabeth collected her coat from Ruth's office, and the two women left the building. It was now getting dark, and Ruth, wanting to go home, said good-bye to the Clerk and walked toward Oxford Street.

Elizabeth paused for a moment on the front steps of the paleontology building to tie her shoe. On an impulse, the Clerk walked around to the north side of the building, looking for the place where bikes were parked when their owners were at work inside. Not only were the bikes easy to find under a floodlight, but Forrest Lang was bending over one, fastening a U-shaped bar of steel through the frame of his bike and around a post. Elizabeth walked over to him. Her appearance at his elbow startled the student into dropping the key. As he bent over to pick it up, Elizabeth said hello. Forrest did not reply.

"Do you always bike?"

"Yes," said Forrest, "if it's any business of yours."

"It's not really. But it will be the police's business at some point. You've let it be known that you weren't here the Sunday before Professor Chadwick was found dead. Isn't that right? You stayed all night Friday but didn't appear again in the labs until Monday morning, shortly after the body was discovered. That's what I've heard. But you know, as much as I'd like to believe you—and I do mean that—it's hard to reconcile that with what is known of your bike's whereabouts."

"What do you mean?" asked Forrest, now clearly on his guard.

"Louis says he was here on Sunday. He didn't see you, because he wasn't on your floor. But your bike was here when he arrived."

Forrest's face lost what little color it had had under the yellow cast of the light. He unstrapped a package from his bike without speaking.

"Maybe your original statement was incomplete," said Elizabeth helpfully. "There could be good reasons for that, other than the one the police might think of."

"Shut up!" said Forrest fiercely, thrusting his face into Elizabeth's. "I don't have to answer anything you say."

Elizabeth stepped back from him. Forrest glared at her for a moment, then strode away around the corner of the paleontology building.

When Elizabeth got home she called Neil Stevenson. This time, he was home. She apologized for being out of touch.

"I gather you've been busy with something," said Neil tensely.

"Yes," said Elizabeth quickly, "and I'm sorry my activities have taken up so much of my time. And of myself. I did try calling you earlier this week, but you weren't home." She regretted her last sentence as soon as she spoke it. It sounded both defensive and lame. "Could I come over and talk, Neil? There are a couple of things lying heavy on my mind these days."

"Of course! Let me come by and pick you up." Neil lived in Belmont, just north of the Cambridge line. Elizabeth was quite capable of driving to his place, but she accepted the offered ride. She knew that Neil did not like her 1977 Chevrolet and worried that it would stall in the middle of traffic circles. Elizabeth was willing to abandon her independence for the moment and accept Neil's old-fashioned ideas of men being the natural drivers and women the natural riders.

Neil's dark blue Buick appeared out in front of Elizabeth's house a few minutes later. He seemed happy to see her, and they chatted about Meeting business as he drove her back to his house. In the kitchen he made her a pot of tea and stirred a cup of instant coffee for himself. He waited patiently for her to speak. He listened quietly and intently to Elizabeth's recounting of Janet's situation at Harvard and was properly alarmed for the young woman. Elizabeth, mindful of what she had learned from Joel Timmermann's response to the same story, did not dwell on Janet's harassment experiences but emphasized instead the complexities of life within the paleontology department. Neil, as always, was a good listener. He empathized and sympathized at the appropriate places. He expressed concern for her safety but managed not to give advice. Elizabeth knew that was rare in a man, and she rewarded her friend with proper affection.

It was only when Neil was driving her back to Concord Avenue that Elizabeth realized she had not mentioned John Anderson. She appreciated Neil's kindness in listening to the story unfolding at Harvard, but she realized she did not trust him to not criticize her welcoming John into her house. She felt too unsure of herself, and of him, to talk about something she found so challenging. At least for the present, she would be silent on that topic.

The same afternoon, but before darkness began to fall, Janet went to her laboratory building to keep an appointment she had with the chairman of her department. Professor Scott's large first floor office was away from the sounds and smells of the laboratories upstairs. He had a Persian carpet on the floor and an overstuffed chair in the corner. As always, Janet felt intimidated by the office accoutrements, but she focused her mind on the task at hand.

"Professor, because of Dr. Chadwick's death, I'll be needing a new advisor. Peter Kolakowski is already on my committee, and that's fine." For as long as he lasts, thought Janet, but continued. "There's really no one else here at Harvard who can read the papers I'll be putting together in the next six months. I'd like Judson at MIT to be on my committee and to be my chief advisor, too."

The chairman looked at Janet narrowly. "The men in your lab are in the same boat. It wouldn't look good for Harvard if all of you asked an MIT prof to advise you."

"Yes, but as it happens, we need his advice. He does the same sort of work that Chadwick did, so he's competent to review our data and theories. And then we'll need three signatures on our theses."

"Actually, although there are three blanks on the form, you only need two professors to sign. I can sign for all of you and Judson or Kolakowski can be the second. When you're done, that is, which may yet be a while." The chairman picked up his Mont Blanc fountain pen and tapped it thoughtfully against his left hand while looking at Janet. "I don't think you've been behaving professionally this year. If your work is similar to your behavior, I doubt anyone will sign your thesis."

The room spun slightly under Janet's feet. "What do you mean?" she asked sharply.

"Whatever was going on between you and Paul

Chadwick was your private business. You had no right to drag the deans into it and make this department look bad. I cannot forget what you did."

Anger flashed through Janet's small frame. "Molestation is never private business!"

"Oh, come now! It was hardly molestation. Everyone knew Paul was a bit of a lech. You only had to say no to what he did. The truth is, you women like the attention."

"That's a crock full of shit and you know it!" cried Janet. "You tolerated it for a generation, and that's your responsibility, not mine. I'm glad I don't have to answer for your actions!"

The chairman was on his feet, as angry as the student before him. "You may have to answer for a lot yourself, young woman! For murder!"

"Nonsense," said Janet with confidence and scorn in her voice. "I wish I had killed him. I congratulate whoever did it! But the thought never occurred to me. He had made me thoroughly sick, and I felt entirely under his thumb. But all that has changed now, and those of you who didn't help me when I asked are going to live to regret it!"

Janet Stevens strode out of the office, slamming the door behind her.

Elizabeth Elliot picked up her mail for the day when Neil dropped her off at home. She found an invitation to dinner on Easter Sunday from her daughter-in-law,

Emily. The time stated was 6 P.M., showing that Emily did not understand that "Sunday dinner" implied a midday meal. It still pained Elizabeth that neither of her sons were Friends and that they observed Easter in un-Quakerly ways. Her elder son, Mark, was a doctor who worked at Children's Hospital in Boston. He had married a pleasant and cheerful woman, and Elizabeth tried to respect his choice. Elizabeth's grandson, Nicky, was being raised without religious life of any kind. As Elizabeth looked at the invitation she longed for the company of her late husband. Neil was a good man, but these children were not his. Her husband, Michael, had always taken a philosophical attitude about the boys. She had worried more and felt unsatisfied at having raised two sons who would never be Quakers.

Then, speaking aloud, Elizabeth reminded herself, "I should be glad to be invited to dinner." She would, of course, accept.

John returned to the Elliot house for supper. He was cheerful and more relaxed than in the morning. Elizabeth listened as he related that the childhood friend he had visited in the morning would be able to give him a job driving a delivery truck.

"Dave's been working for UPS since high school. He's sort of a foreman, now. He thinks he can get me the job driving from here to Maine and back each day. No deliveries, just over-the-road driving."

Elizabeth expressed her delight that he already had a lead for a job.

"And I went to see my parole officer, too. To get

out of prison I told them I could stay with my dad. And Dad wrote out a letter for me, saying that was OK. But we always fight, and I know I'd be kicked out of the house within a week, so I'm glad to stay here while I get things set up for myself. I told the parole guy I was at home, and things were fine. It'd be a violation of my parole to live anywhere else, you see. He'd never understand who you are or why I'm here. And I said that I didn't need his help with a job 'cause I'd got something lined up with UPS. So I don't have to go back and see him for six weeks."

Elizabeth felt qualms at the dishonesty of which she was now a part. But then, she had tacitly encouraged Louis to look at things in his advisor's office, and she had allowed Ruth to let her into another man's office only today. The Clerk's activities this week were far different from John's supposed crime, but not so different from his current manipulation of the truth.

I have good reasons for what I've done, thought Elizabeth defensively, even if it's all wrong.

CHAPTER ELEVEN

I had fainted, unless I had believed to see the goodness of the Lord in the land of the living.

PSALM 27:13

"This is it," Louis said with satisfaction. "It's been two years of work, but I've got a model now that explains not only my data but several of those big papers by Chadwick et al. that you and I had to study when we first came here." Louis was sitting at the little table next to the department's coffeepot holding forth to Eric and Forrest.

"Oh, really?" asked the latter. "When will you get it out to a journal?"

"In a couple of months. I've got to finish up something in the lab for Peter, so that will slow me down. But I've got everything in my notebook, and, when I get several free weeks, I'll move it to the word processor and send it to *Science*. It's going to change our views," said Louis rising from his place.

"Congratulations," said Eric with a smile. "Be sure and give me a signed reprint."

"You bet!" responded Louis, sauntering out of the coffee room.

At 9 P.M. that evening, Louis entered the locked laboratory room belonging to Peter Kolakowski. Peter's office down the hall was dark; he had gone home. Louis turned on his small flashlight and turned out the main lights in the room. In the darkness he walked over to his bench, looked at his line of notebooks on the shelf above his work area, and sighed. He had no idea if Elizabeth Elliot's plan would work.

Moving to the west wall of the lab, he spread the emergency fire blanket on the linoleum tiles and curled up on top of it. The bed was uncomfortable; he knew he would sleep little, if at all. Time passed slowly in the dark laboratory. The fume hood fan whirred and clanked, a freezer in the corner cycled on and off, and a siren in the distance wailed down Oxford Street.

Shortly after midnight, just as Louis was stiffening into what he feared might be a permanently crippled state, he heard a sound from the hallway. Louis's ears had become used to the sounds within the lab, and he unconsciously filtered them out. What he heard now were clearly footfalls. A key slid into the lock. Louis was aware when the door opened because he felt a fresh draft. Then he heard the door quietly click shut. The beam of a flashlight shone across the room, and a figure moved toward Louis's bench.

The flashlight's swath of light moved up to Louis's shelf. A hand began to take notebooks off the shelf and set them down on the bench counter. Louis slowly crawled toward the hall, moving silently and glad of the time to limber up his stiff joints. He reached the door, under which he could see the faint light of the emergency bulbs in the hallway, and stood up. He switched on the room lights and turned in the bright glare. At Louis's bench stood Forrest Lang, blinking in surprise.

"So that was the result, Mrs. Elliot," said Louis over the telephone the next morning. "He threatened me by saying he'd expose Peter. He said that would ruin my career, too, and he'd gladly do it if I mentioned to anybody that he reads other people's things at night. Then he stalked out of the room. I had some rather strong things in mind to say to him, but since he's bigger than me, I let him go. Anyway, it's clear that Forrest is in the habit of reading other people's notes and papers."

"I'm sure that's unprofessional. But is it unethical? I mean, would scientists think it similar to fabricating data?"

"Not at all," answered Louis. "It shows he's scum. But reading other people's papers that are left in a lab isn't what you'd call a cardinal sin."

Elizabeth did not understand any demarcation system for the magnitude of sins, so she let the remark pass.

"As for the other matter you asked me to look into," said Louis, "I'm not sure how you got interested in Eric's senior theses, but there does seem to be a problem with it. I asked him for a copy, saying I wanted to read up on that area. He got awfully strange and said it wasn't worth my while. I kept after him, and eventually he said he no longer had a copy. That's got to be wrong. All those Princeton boys are terribly proud of their senior theses. They all have to write them, and you'd think they each invented the wheel the way they talk about their undergraduate research. He has a copy bound in Corinthian leather, I'm sure, but for some reason he won't lend it to me."

"Thanks very much," said Elizabeth.

"I could get a copy from Princeton on interlibrary loan if you really want to see it, but that'll take a couple of weeks."

"No thank you, Louis, that's not necessary. I know you didn't get much sleep last night, but I've a technical problem I was wondering if you could help me with." She explained about the unintentional engravings on Paul Chadwick's Post-it Note. "I can read a few of the words, and I'm sure the note's addressed to your advisor. But a lot of it is faint and it's all in tiny script."

"Well the size is no problem. I can photograph it with some bright lights off to one side and then enlarge the print," said Louis.

"I don't know anything about such things, but if we could decipher this it might clear up a lot. But do you have photographic equipment?"

"Not mine personally. But we have lots of stuff in the department. We use photography a lot in lab work, and it's one of the things I'm best at. I'd be happy to work on a nice little technical matter. It'll take my mind off my professional future and the group meeting talk I'm supposed to give to everyone in Chadwick's and Kolakowski's lab this Friday. With all the recent excitement, I'm afraid my work hasn't been advancing much. So I'll come over to your house this evening, if that's OK, and have a look at the note."

Elizabeth agreed and said she would expect him.

Elizabeth was just sitting down for her afternoon tea the following day when John returned. He had departed in the morning without saying a word. Now he smelled of alcohol and walked in short, carefully controlled, steps.

"Afternoon," he said cheerfully. He sat down heavily at the kitchen table.

"Oh, John!" Elizabeth could not refrain from exclaiming. "Have you been drinking?" The Clerk, like most Quakers, regarded all alcoholic beverages as temptation. To make things worse, John's clothes reeked of smoke, and she involuntarily made a face at the smell.

He saw the grimace. "Not at all. Had a beer with an old friend, that's all. Down at the Stag in Central Square."

"In the middle of the day?" blurted the Quaker. She knew that non-Quakers made a distinction between daytime and nighttime drinking and hoped John might share part of that sensibility.

"And why not?" answered John, now becoming angry. "Jesus Christ, in prison I had more freedom!"

Elizabeth sat upright and looked directly at him. "John Anderson, I won't be spoken to in that tone of voice and with that language in my own house. Not by anyone! I won't have people who stay with me come home swearing. Swearing because they're drunk!"

Elizabeth's voice became much stronger as she spoke. John sat for a moment in silence, taking her in. In a gentler tone the Quaker added, "Maybe you could go upstairs and lie down."

"Just what I had in mind when I came in," replied John. He stood up. "You know, it's not a crime to have a beer and maybe even swear once a day. You distrust me, I know, but you might cut a guy a little slack now and then. I'm not a demon, just a regular fellow. I don't smoke around here because you asked me not to, and I didn't bring any beer back with me. That's more than a lot of men could manage." He walked slowly out of the room.

Elizabeth was distressed, but her mind was jerked back to the Harvard situation when the doorbell rang. It was Louis. After a quick look at the note Elizabeth had taken from the university, he said he thought he could decipher it that same evening. Elizabeth and he agreed he would call her with news of what it said. He departed, and just before nine o'clock, he called. The message on the note was exactly the sort of thing Elizabeth had expected. She talked to Louis about his group meeting on the next day and asked him to allow her to usurp his time as speaker.

"While everyone in the labs is gathered together, I'd like to talk to them. As a group, we can sort several things out. I want the men in your department to understand what the situation has been so that those who have been in the wrong can turn themselves in to the police. Before the weekend I should explain to Detective Burnham how and why the murder was committed, but I'd like the wrongdoers to have to confront each other and themselves. It may shock them into taking responsibility for what they've done. That will be crucial to their souls."

"You don't want to fill me in now about all this?" asked Louis hopefully.

"No. I may be wrong in what I've conjectured, and I want to see everyone's response to what I have to say. We'll learn tomorrow what the story is."

Louis agreed to cooperate and Elizabeth gave him instructions about something she wanted him to bring to the meeting in addition to the note. After hanging up, Elizabeth called the police station and got Detective Burnham's home telephone number. She reached him thoro.

"This is Elizabeth Elliot. I'm sorry to disturb you at home, but I want you to be aware of something that will happen at the paleontology department tomorrow. It's relevant to your case."

"Shoot."

"I think I understand both who committed the murder and what other wrongs have been done in that building—in addition to sexual harassment, that is. Tomorrow I can clear it all up, God willing. I'd like you to come to Harvard in case any of the men involved in this case want to turn themselves in."

"You expect a confession? You have no authority to even question them!"

"There are several sorts of authority in the world, Mr. Burnham. I have had sufficient authority, it would appear, to solve this mystery. I'd like you there because I am hopeful that after everyone knows the truth, the wrongdoers will want to speak to you. It's their best hope, from a legal standpoint I'm sure, and I know it would be the best for them as humans. If you could come to Ruth Markham's office at three fifteen, I think I can promise you an end to this case."

"I doubt it, but perhaps those guys have said more to you as a civilian than they have to me. I'll come to the secretary's office not because I think you can frighten them into confessions, but because I have things to check on there. I've been looking through the financial records of Professor Chadwick's lab. Nothing irregular so far, but normal police procedure dictates I look at everything, and I have a lot left to wade through."

"Fine. I'm glad you'll be there. I'll come to Ruth's office by four P.M."

CHAPTER TWELVE

My God, my God, why hast thou forsaken me?
PSALMS 22:1

On the morning of Good Friday, the Clerk of Friends Meeting at Cambridge got up and dressed. The door to Andy's old bedroom stood open. John and his few belongings were gone. Downstairs on the kitchen table the Clerk found the spare house key she had given him. There was no note.

The Quaker sat down to her tea and toast with a leaden spirit. She had not meant to make John feel he must leave. But she could not tolerate, in her own house, behavior from him which she would not have allowed from her sons.

"It was wrong of me to invite him here," she said to herself, shaking her head sadly. "My way of life is so peculiar, no normal person could fit into it. I hope he can understand I meant well."

Elizabeth's cat, whom she had barely seen during John's visit, rubbed against her ankles and then leapt up to a chair to keep her mistress company.

"I intended no harm," she said to Sparkle. "But I did fly off the handle about the beer, I suppose. I don't think alcohol is necessarily evil, but I'm glad Michael and I always followed Friends' tradition and abstained." The Quaker reflected on the number of people she knew who had been harmed by alcohol. Some lives were completely destroyed by the drug. This juncture in John's life was so important, she wished he would stay away from all danger, including beer drinking. Caution is what she would choose for him. "But then, it's not my choice. And he may feel bitter and rejected," said Elizabeth to the cat. "Ralph understands these things better than I do. Perhaps even Andrew does. I shouldn't have meddled."

The cat looked at the Clerk mutely.

"I'll go down to Central Square, to The Stag, and just see if John is there. Maybe I could apologize."

The Quaker skipped her breakfast in her haste to take action. Forgetting to feed either Sparkle or the birds, she walked down Concord Avenue to Harvard Square. The Red Line carried Elizabeth to Central Square and she found The Stag immediately. It was a dark and smelly bar, full of men even at this hour of the day. Elizabeth summoned her courage. She asked the bartender if he had seen John Anderson.

"Yup, he's in the corner."

Elizabeth saw John and crossed over to him. He had a sandwich in front of him and a half-full bottle of beer. He looked up but waited for her to speak.

"I'm glad I found you. I came to say I'm sorry if I seemed unreasonable."

He looked thoughtfully at her before slowly saying, "Not so much unreasonable as distrustful."

Elizabeth considered. In the nature of things, she was distrustful of anyone convicted of any form of rape. She thought, however, that distrust had not guided her actions.

"I'm sorry that it seemed I didn't trust you, or that I don't like you. That's not true."

"Look, I did my best to fit into your house, OK? But I called Ralph Park last night and talked it out with him. It's not too much to expect to be able to smoke and have a beer. That's normal. It's not as if I was bringing coke into your house. I told him I was going back to my father's place. My dad's a son of a bitch in a lot of ways, but his house will be a better place for me than yours. I'll feel at home, if you know what I mean."

"You're still welcome with me."

"Welcome to what? To be treated like a pariah? My dad and I will be at each other's throats, but we'll be on equal terms. He's sure not holier-than-thou. And that looks good to me." John took a large bite of his sandwich and stared down into his beer.

Elizabeth thought for a moment and then said, "I'm sorry I made you feel unwelcome. Old Quaker ladies are a peculiar breed, I'm sure. I hope that you'll keep in touch with Ralph. The Meeting may be able to be more useful than I have been."

John took another bite out of his sandwich and grunted.

"Good-bye," said Elizabeth and turned away. She

was relieved to leave the dark bar and return to the sunlight outside.

Tears welled up in the Clerk's eyes as she blinked in the light. Perhaps she should have discussed this with Neil, who could have provided a man's perspective on the situation. But Elizabeth had tried to do what she thought was right. Her tears slowed and, taking firm hold of herself, she crossed Massachusetts Avenue and went back into the darkness of the subway. She had a long wait on the platform, and as she waited her tears dried on her cheek.

The train pulled in and Elizabeth boarded the last car. The car was crowded, but a young man gave her his seat in the corner. She accepted his old-fashioned offer and gratefully sat down just as the train began to accelerate. One minute later, with a loud clang, the car sharply slowed down. A woman's voice over the loudspeaker announced that the train was "experiencing difficulties." What a way to speak of the subway, thought Elizabeth, as if it were human.

The cars remained stationary in the darkness for some time. The minutes passed slowly, with the car growing steadily stuffier. A middle-aged man holding onto a strap reached out and took the wrist of a young woman sitting three persons down from Elizabeth. She was neither good-looking nor plain, just a normal woman in her twenties with long hair in a braid down her back. The man began to talk intensely to her. She shook her head and looked away from him, but her wrist remained in his grasp.

"Are you a student?" asked the man repeatedly,

drawing her hand down toward his pocket. She successfully pulled her hand away from him and again shook her head. She looked down at the floor of the car and said nothing. He continued to talk to her, asking if she lived in Cambridge and where she had come from before that. He told her his name and asked what hers was. Again she shook her head and was silent. She moved a foot down the bench on which she was sitting. Then, apparently afraid he might sit down beside her in the small gap her movement had created, she scooted back to where she had been. The man persisted in asking her name.

Discomfort at this scene was felt by all the people in the rear section of the car, but no one had interrupted what was happening. Finally, Elizabeth shook off her paralysis and began to rise to her feet, the better to interpose herself between the man and the young woman. Just as she did so, however, the train lurched forward, toppling her down into her seat. As a sixty-six-year-old, she did not relish the thought of standing up while the train was picking up speed. The man, for his part, grabbed a pole a few feet away from the woman for support as the train accelerated. As the train pulled into the Harvard Square station, the young woman scrambled to the nearest door and was out of the car as soon as the door opened. Her braided hair disappeared into the crowd in a moment. Elizabeth was glad she had escaped but sorry she and the others around her had not responded to what had occurred.

She thinks no one cared, that no one felt her shame, thought the Quaker as she left the car and slowly climbed the stairway that led up to the gates of Harvard Yard. It was mid-morning. The sun was high enough in the sky to remind even an arthritic, discouraged Quaker of the coming blessings of summer. But as Elizabeth walked back up Concord Avenue, her mood did not improve. She prayed that both John Anderson and the young woman might come to understand that not everyone wished them ill. Still, she knew she had failed them both.

Harvard took no holiday on the day memorializing the crucifixion, but at noon a number of students and staff excused themselves to go to services. St. Paul's had a somber observance, and the faithful turned out to see the stations of the cross remembered. Louis Lazier went to the early part of the service. He had only partially adapted to recent events. It was only last Sunday that he had held a palm in his hand, looking for the first time at the facts of his advisor's duplicity. Now he felt that, whatever he must pay for exposing Peter's fraud, he had done the right thing. In the morning he had written out all that he knew, documenting it with photocopies of Peter's articles, and left everything with the chairman's secretary. She had said that Professor Scott was out of town but would be back at Harvard on Monday. Louis made it clear to her the papers were important and should be on the top of his mail when he returned. Although it had been a wrenching morning, Louis knew there was no way he could have remained silent.

Louis knelt and tried to keep his mind on the readings. Everything about Catholic ritual was familiar and comforting, reminding him of better days when he was a child. At the end of a long passage of Scripture, Louis slipped out of his pew and walked quietly up the aisle and out of doors. He was scheduled to give a group meeting talk at three o'clock. He had no talk prepared, but Elizabeth Elliot had said she would come. She had assured him that she was so well prepared he would not need to speak at all.

Louis entered the conference room on the second floor of the paleontology building with his book bag over his shoulder and a stack of papers under his arm. It was one minute before three o'clock. He set the bag down on a vacant chair and the papers on the table. Peter Kolakowski and Eric Townsend were seated at the long table in the center of the room, deep in a discussion about the mass spectrometer. Eric's personal radio hung around his neck. Forrest Lang entered on Louis's heels, followed by Janet Stevens. A moment later, Elizabeth Elliot came in.

A ripple of surprise spread over the room as the newcomer sat down at the head of the table. She nodded to Louis.

"This was supposed to be a talk about my research this past semester," began Louis, "but it's going to be something quite different." He glanced around and added, "It'll be more interesting than my data, I'm sure."

"I want a chance to speak to all of you," said Elizabeth, "and Louis has been kind enough to give me his time slot here."

"Mrs. Elliot, isn't it?" said Peter with a smile, "this is hardly your place, ma'am."

"No, it's not," responded the Quaker, "and I'll be happy to leave this building for good this afternoon. But it's to everyone's advantage that I be here now. Several of you have deeply transgressed. At least two of you could face criminal charges. It will benefit you to listen to what I have to say if only because the police always look more favorably on people who turn themselves in." As she said this she saw Ruth Markham in the hallway. Ruth quietly took up a place leaning against the doorjam, neither in nor out of the room.

"You've certainly got our attention," said Eric. "A group meeting to be remembered!"

"As you know, Janet Stevens had submitted a personal complaint against Professor Chadwick last month. It was because of that action that I came to know her. She was with me on the morning that Mr. Chadwick's body was discovered."

"Women do stick together," drawled Forrest.

"Maybe, but perhaps we have to," answered Elizabeth. "In any event, what I've discovered in this department has proven that Janet is not guilty."

Elizabeth turned toward Eric Townsend and held him with a searching look. "Tell us the truth, Eric. What were you doing here so early on Sunday morning, the day before the body was discovered?"

Eric looked extremely uncomfortable. Involuntarily he glanced at Forrest as he replied, "I was just finishing up some sample preparations."

"So early on a Sunday? With a wife and a fine apartment to enjoy in Newton?" queried Janet.

"Speaking of your wife, I understand she's an MBA, employed in downtown Boston," said Elizabeth.

"Yes," said Eric. "She's at State Street Bank. But I don't see what difference that makes."

"State Street is doing well even in these difficult times," said Elizabeth. "Yet you're teaching an undergraduate class for the money and borrowing more on a student loan program. What's the problem with your cash flow?"

"Nothing!" stammered Eric.

"Forrest, meanwhile, is doing well without work and loans, buying new, deluxe computers. You've been giving money to Forrest, haven't you, Eric?" asked Elizabeth gently. For a moment, the room was as silent as a Quaker meeting. "It's not a crime to be blackmailed. Whatever's wrong with your senior thesis can't be worse than the suspicion of murder."

"Why suspect me of murder?" asked Eric hotly.

"Paul Chadwick had your Princeton thesis on his desk when he died. He was looking into it. You had planned to publish it and some related work you did here last fall, didn't you?"

"He did," said Janet. "I remember he told me about it."

"Yes, and he told Louis. And no doubt you, too, Forrest."

Forrest glared at Elizabeth and said "Don't say anything, Townsend. You don't have to say a word to this old bitch."

"No, you don't," said Elizabeth. "But when I speak to the police, they'll be looking into why Professor Chadwick had taken an interest in your old work. They'll want to know what's wrong with it and what would have happened to your career if he had exposed you. What was the trouble? Did you make up your data?"

"No!" shouted Eric hotly. "I've never done anything like that!" He continued more calmly with a glance at Forrest. "It's almost a relief to tell the truth. Part of the last chapter in my thesis was plagiarized. It was spring of my senior year, and I had lots to do, what with finishing up classes and visiting graduate schools here in New England. I copied from several sources and didn't reference them. But that didn't affect my data and my interpretations! The work is good; it's only the text in the last chapter that's regrettable. Mrs. Elliot, this is the truth. I didn't know Chadwick had my senior thesis!" Eric looked at Forrest. "Did you sell me out despite all I paid you?"

"Shut up!" snarled Forrest.

"Blackmail is a crime, Forrest," said Elizabeth evenly. "Even though it pays well."

"Did you get the money for your new Mac from Eric?" said Louis, looking at Forrest derisively.

"You're a lower form of life than anything yet discovered."

"I did come in early on Sunday, Mrs. Elliot," said Eric more calmly. "Not to pay him any more, but to tell him I didn't have a cent more to give. I said he could expose me if he wanted. It was plagiarism, but it was only part of one chapter of my thesis. The degree would never have been revoked, and I decided I could live with the damage to my reputation. If need be, I'd leave science and do something new rather than have this parasite bleed me to death."

The Quaker nodded her head. She looked around the room.

"Forrest is in the habit of reading everything that is recorded around here," said Elizabeth. "Paul Chadwick's office was disturbed before his death. He blamed Ruth Markham for rearranging his papers, but it was you, wasn't it Forrest?"

Forrest said nothing.

"After I told you guys this week about the new theory I was onto," said Louis, "I stayed all night in our lab upstairs. Sure enough, Forrest here showed up to read my notebooks."

Forrest still said nothing.

"And you read Janet's lab notebooks at some point since she's been away. You put them back in order left to right, but she keeps them right to left," said Elizabeth.

"Reading things that people leave in labs is not illegal," said Forrest.

"But it stinks!" interjected Janet.

"Where does this leave us, Mrs. Elliot?" asked Peter. "Are you saying Eric is the murderer because he didn't want to be exposed?"

"No, another person has been guilty of more than plagiarism. Would you explain the details, Louis?"

"I'm sorry, Peter," said Louis, "but somebody's got to do this." He picked up the papers he had earlier placed on the table and handed one each around the room, even including Ruth at the door. "This is a list I compiled of your articles, Professor."

"I can see that," said Peter stiffly.

"I've summarized the type and quantity of data that the articles are based on. All of the data were supposedly gathered by you."

Eric shook his head. "I didn't realize it was so much. I've never seen it all brought together in one place."

"Nor had I," said Louis, "until Mrs. Elliot put me onto this. It's clearly impossible for one man to have done it all."

"People work at different rates," said Peter in a low voice.

"Yes, but nobody can get this much isotope data produced in such a brief time. On the other hand," said Louis, "if the data are fabricated, it'd be easy enough to write up articles to present them."

"Jesus!" said Eric. "Could he really get away with it?"

"Has anybody tried to duplicate these numbers?" asked Louis.

"No," said Eric thoughtfully. "Why waste time re-doing basic lab work?"

"Exactly. We proceed on trust around here. We don't even consider the possibility that somebody is a thorough-going liar. That's why he got away with it for so long."

"Except for Forrest Lang," Elizabeth broke in. "Who trusts no one. You read Peter's notebooks, didn't you? Or did you just read the published articles and realize the data were too numerous to be credible?"

"Or maybe you stumbled across an identical data set I found in Peter's stuff," said Louis, looking at Forrest. "Two columns of numbers, supposedly about completely different things, but with each number identical?"

"That can't be true!" broke in Peter.

"But it is. You're not just a cheat, you're sloppy about it!" said Louis angrily.

"He's sloppy," said Forrest quietly. "It was the duplicated data set that I first noticed. That got me started looking at all of his data more closely. You think I'm scum, Louis, because of forcing money out of Eric. But his wife makes lots, and I needed it for my work. Peter is worse than dirt. He's been making up data his whole career."

"No," said Peter shaking his head, "That's not true."

"It is true," said Louis quietly. "I've written all this out for the chairman. He'll read it when he comes back to town on Monday."

"Your whole career hasn't been a fraud," said Elizabeth gently. "In graduate school it wasn't, was it? Only here at Harvard where you were under pressure to get tenure."

Peter was silent.

"And Forrest knew everything and took advantage of it?" asked Janet, looking at Elizabeth.

"Why did Forrest get that special postdoc at MIT for next year?" Elizabeth asked Peter. "I heard you had moved heaven and earth to get him a place. Not just because you were sorry his advisor had died, surely? You've done nothing similar for Janet or Eric, after all."

Janet asked of no one in particular, "Forrest threatened to expose Peter, didn't he? So Peter wrote him a letter of recommendation saying he was the best paleontologist the world had ever seen?"

"That's right. But the unresolved question in my mind was why Dr. Chadwick was in his lab when the gas was released, and who could have known he would be there. There was a Post-it Note attached to something Paul Chadwick gave you," said Elizabeth, still intent on Peter. "Louis was kind enough to help me read the sheet immediately underneath. The writing made indentations, you see. All I could read was that he'd written: 'Peter: This is a list of something-something-something and I want to something-something-something.' "

"Mrs. Elliot asked for my help," said Louis. "I took a photo of the paper with our strongest photographic lamps all off to one side. It highlighted the indentations with shadow. And I blew up a print, since Chadwick always wrote so small."

"Even I could read it then," said Elizabeth. "It said: 'Peter: This is a list of the data contained in your articles of the last five years. It's literally incredible and I want to meet with you in my lab at 4 o'clock on Sunday.' I don't know why that time and place were chosen. Maybe he wanted to give you some privacy and figured few people would be around on Sunday afternoon. His office is so small and cramped, I understand he often met with people in the lab, isn't that so?"

Louis and Janet nodded.

"So you knew what was coming, didn't you?" continued Elizabeth quietly. "Forrest spent Friday night in the labs 'pulling an all-nighter,' as you say, keeping up with his nocturnal readings. You couldn't do anything then. But on Saturday night you were here. There were valves and a timer above Janet's bench. You recognized the company names and you got the boxes down. It was easy to add a timer valve to the end of the oxygen line. You set it for four-oh-five or so the next day.

"You hoped it would look like an accident, didn't you? Not a rational hope, perhaps, but you're not a murderer by nature," said Elizabeth to Peter. He looked at the table in front of him and said nothing. "But the trouble was, the line has its complexities. Two of the valves between the canister, when it's hooked up, and the outside world are manual. There's a timer only on the last valve. Nobody leaves the manual valves open—at least that's what the students tell me."

"Of course not," said Eric. "That would be asking for an accident."

"That's what you all explained to Detective Burnham when he asked about the line, isn't that right?"

Eric nodded his head.

"And so," continued Elizabeth, "the detective knew there had been foul play."

"Peter went to New York early on Sunday, the timer ticking away. When he returned to Logan Airport here in Boston on Monday morning, he came into work, well after the early morning hours when the body would be discovered by a student, a janitor, or a secretary."

"Jesus!" swore Eric.

Elizabeth observed to the room at large: "Peter Kolakowski is not a thoroughly vicious man, any more than Paul Chadwick. Paul had intellectual integrity in a way several people around here don't. And Peter would never have killed if his cheating had not been discovered."

"But Eric could have done all that you say Peter did, to prevent his plagiarism from being exposed," said Louis softly.

"His going away for the day is what made it clear Peter was the murderer, not Eric," said Elizabeth. "Eric volunteered he was here on Sunday. Not in his lab, but in his office. He'd seen Forrest, and he said so. But you were safely in New York, Peter—too safely. Eric didn't do anything, did he? You did all the work on Saturday night, isn't that right?"

"Goddamn you!" shouted Peter springing to his feet.

"That's our answer," said Ruth calmly from the doorway.

"Paul Chadwick was living slime," said Louis to Peter. "But you didn't kill him because of that. You murdered him for your chance at tenure!"

"Don't sneer at me, kid!" said Peter. "You're never going to make it in the big leagues. Don't forget, I'm your advisor, I know your work. You don't cut it, but I did! I had as much right to tenure as Paul Chadwick did in his day. He came along in the sixties when standards for paleo were low. I don't apologize for anything!"

"Let me repeat," said Elizabeth quietly, "that anybody who has broken the law is treated more leniently if they turn themselves in."

"But you'll do the work for us if we don't cooperate, isn't that right?" said Forrest with a sneer.

"You would help yourselves by admitting to the police what you have done. And Detective Burnham is in Ruth's office right now if you want to speak to him."

"Goddamn you all!" said Peter. He strode out of the room, barely giving Ruth time to move out of his way.

Forrest Lang stood and left silently.

Elizabeth put her head in her hands for a minute until Janet asked if she were all right.

"Yes," said the Quaker, "I think so. Let me go

down the hall and see if Detective Burnham has company."

Ruth stepped fully into the room and said, "I'll wait here. You know me, always discreet."

"You'll need this," said Louis. "I did what you said and turned it on before I came here." He stepped over to the chair along the wall and leaned over his bookbag. He opened the bag and took out a tape recorder. "It's still purring along," he said. Elizabeth took it from him with thanks after he had shut it off.

Elizabeth Elliot was sharply disappointed to find Detective Burnham alone. He was seated at Ruth's desk looking at ledgers, but he glanced up when she came in. The Clerk closed the door behind her and said tiredly, "Has no one been here to speak to you?"

"No. What have you been doing, Mrs. Elliot?"

Elizabeth sat down slowly and tried to smile at the detective. "Thank you very much for coming, nonetheless. I wanted a couple of the men here to be able to talk to you of their own accord, before they had too much time to calculate consequences. But if they won't, I think it's my responsibility to give you this." She handed him the tape recorder and explained that it contained the record of the conversation that had just occurred down the hall.

"You confronted them with your ideas, but they said nothing, eh?" asked Burnham.

"On the contrary," said Elizabeth, "they told everything. That didn't surprise me. But I'm sorry they didn't have the courage to face you right now. I believe that the killer, at least, might have eventually confessed to everything, no matter if both you and I were unable to solve this murder."

"If you've helped my office to understand the situation here, I'll be glad. Our methods are different, but I admit I respect your results. No policeman can catch people off their guard like a civilian can. We have to be objective in our thinking, and we must always proceed by the book."

"My thinking about the paleontology department has been objective, but I had the advantage over you of getting to know Janet and Louis personally. They told me a number of things that I could piece together one, and only one, way. You'll find it all on the tape."

"Can you wait here while I listen?" asked the Detective peering at the little machine.

"Of course," said the Quaker.

Detective Burnham rewound Louis's tape. The recording was not the best, but everyone's words were audible. Elizabeth identified the speakers at first, but Burnham waved her to stop, muttering that he could tell who was who. When the tape ended, Burnham stood up and said, "You shouldn't have let Kolakowski and Lang have a head start! I'll get a warrant for the blackmailer as soon as I can, but the first thing to do is run down Kolakowski. God alone knows where he is by now."

"God does know, of course," said Elizabeth. "I doubt the professor has gone far. Try his office upstairs."

Burnham left Ruth's room and hurried up the stairway. Elizabeth heard the big man negotiating the steps three at a time. She walked back to the conference room. Eric was gone, but Ruth, Louis, and Janet were there, waiting for her. She explained what had transpired in Ruth's office.

"So!" said Ruth. "You've solved this crime—or should I say crimes—and that cop didn't even thank you! Is that typical of men or what?"

"Let's not be hard on all men," said Elizabeth, "and detectives have to behave like policemen. It's part of their job." She motioned for the others to stand up and said, "I need to get out of this building. It's oppressive."

"I've got to stay," said Ruth. "But you're looking like a corpse, Elizabeth. You'd better go home. I'll call you tomorrow, OK? Just to see how you are."

"I'll gladly go home," said the Clerk. She and Janet and Louis walked downstairs slowly. A moment later the threesome stepped out the front door of the paleontology building. All of them were glad to leave behind the world of laboratories and fluorescent lights and breathe in the sun and wind of a New England spring day.

"We'll walk you home, Mrs. Elliot. You really do look pale," said Janet. "It's trite to say, but I know I owe you a lot. And I'll never forget what you've done. Thanks so much!"

"I'm glad I was at the Meetinghouse when you came by that day."

"Perhaps it was providential."

"Since a Quaker saved your skin," said Louis with

a smile, "I'm afraid you may be spending more and more time with Friends in the future."

"I'll save time for one Catholic," replied Janet, holding out her hand to Louis. He took the offered hand quickly, and the trio walked abreast across the law school yard toward Concord Avenue. "You know, Louis, I've been thinking. Neither of us has the proper credentials to continue in academic work. We lack letters of recommendation from our advisors."

"We lack more than letters! We don't even have advisors! Mine's under arrest, and your's is under the sod!"

"True. So what we need to do is face up to that. Change our goals! We should finish up these degrees and then do something different. Go into banking or politics or write novels."

"A change does seem like a good idea," said Louis, too lightly to be fully credible. He added, "I could go into the priesthood."

"No! That's a lousy thought!"

Even Elizabeth laughed. She said, "The way will open up for you two, I'm sure. I'm sorry that your scientific careers have been damaged by the situation in this terrible department of yours, but you're young and bright and, with time, I trust you'll both find some way to be paleontologists if that's what you want to pursue. Your paths in your profession, of course, may have to be different from what you imagined when you enrolled at Harvard. But you both have time to become what you wish. I shall pray it will work out for you both."

*   *   *

Holy Saturday dawned dark, damp, and cool. There
were no special services at St. Paul's, but throughout
the morning people came for individual prayer as they
awaited the resurrection. Elizabeth slept until dawn,
when arthritic pain awakened her. She had breakfast
in a kitchen that seemed empty without John Anderson. She took a double dose of arthritis medicine. Her
head began to hurt shortly thereafter, and she returned
to bed. She felt dejected and empty. Her headache
increased, and soon the pain became throbbing and
intense. She realized she was going into a migraine
attack. She took the strongest narcotic she had from
the doctor, pulled down the shades in her room, unplugged the phone, and pulled the covers over her
head. She remembered that Ruth had promised to call
to check up on her, but she did not want to speak to
anyone. Not to Neil, not even to her children. In the
quiet and dark room the narcotics took hold and her
head pain eased.

In the afternoon she regained a hazy sort of consciousness. Her mind was thick and slow, but her head
was free of pain. She lay still and tried to think what
day of the week it was. Then she remembered all the
events of Friday.

That's why I'm feeling so ill, she thought to herself. All that responsibility has come to an end. I did
what I did and now it's over. Both at Harvard and
here with John, it's all over.

Nothing Elizabeth had done for John Anderson had turned out right, and she regretted she had not discussed that situation with Neil. But then she remembered how distraught Janet had been when they first met at Meeting, and she felt warm joy that the young woman was now out of danger and back on the road to health.

"Comfort ye, comfort ye my people, saith your God," recollected Elizabeth from Isaiah, happy to apply the verse to herself. The sun was shining outside, and the blinds glowed yellow in the afternoon light. Her arthritic pains had gone, and she knew the intense headache would not return. She dozed off.

CHAPTER THIRTEEN

Shew me thy ways, O Lord; teach me thy paths.
PSALM 25:4

At 1:45 A.M. Elizabeth Elliot awoke with sharp pains in her shoulders. She listened to the rain for a moment, but the pain which had awakened her soon took her attention away from the sounds of the weather. Lying in the darkness, she resolved to go back to her old arthritis medicine for a while, even though it was injurious to her stomach. The new prescription didn't reduce her joint pain enough to make rainstorms tolerable. And in New England, no one could count on dry weather.

An hour later the Clerk was still awake. Her head felt fine but her weight-bearing joints were in pain. It was impossible for her to stop thinking, with regret, about many of her actions within the paleontology department and with John Anderson. The rain had stopped. Rising and moving slowly to the bathroom, she took a codeine tablet. She paused for a moment at the bathroom window to look out into the darkness.

Everything was still. She returned to bed, where she quickly drifted off into a hazy dream of her children at play in the backyard.

Had Elizabeth looked out her front window rather than the rear one, she might have seen a well-dressed man walking down Concord Avenue. Andrew Elliot, her younger son, walked briskly, oppressed neither by the damp nor the complete darkness. He looked fondly at his parents' house. His mother had called him on Friday evening to report that John Anderson had left for good. Andrew had done his best to suppress his relief and satisfaction. Because the only light Elizabeth had turned on shone out into the backyard, he saw nothing amiss in his mother's house as he passed by. Walking through the quiet and deserted streets, he cut across to Longfellow Park and turned downriver along Memorial Drive.

His purposefulness was clear in his stride and in his Sunday clothes. Andrew had slept even less than his mother, but he was determined to use the remainder of the night in a special way. Over a ten-minute period, as Elizabeth fell more deeply into a drug-induced sleep, other Episcopalians and Anglicans appeared in the darkness of Memorial Drive. Most of them were carefully dressed, but a few had plainly been turned out of bed in the middle of the night. They followed Andrew's footsteps and went into the monastery on the Charles River to begin their annual Easter vigil.

Some of the monks had been keeping a vigil straight through the night. Lay people were invited within the monastery walls on this special night only after 3:00 A.M. Taking their places around the altar at the front of the sanctuary, they sat or kneeled in silence. They began to pray with the brothers and await sunup and the resurrection. Elizabeth, by this time, was deep under the influence of her codeine, quite oblivious of the importance of the hour.

Well after sunrise, Elizabeth awoke to the sound of her clock radio. The sun shone in through her bedroom window. The arthritis pain had eased while she slept, and she got out of bed without wincing.

It's Sunday, she thought to herself. And I have care of first Meeting. She shook the heaviness out of her head and dressed. Then she breakfasted and replenished the bird feeder outside the kitchen window. She was glad that the rain of the night was over. The sun was out, the world looked and smelled fresh, and her joints were not a torment anymore.

It was not until she was walking down Concord Avenue toward the Meeting that Elizabeth realized it was Easter Sunday. She thought of it because there were well-dressed people walking up and down the avenue. On a regular Sunday, Elizabeth met only the homeless on the streets around the common, but on Easter many Cambridge residents made their annual visit to a church, sporting new clothes.

When Elizabeth arrived at the Meetinghouse she noted that the crowd was no larger than normal. The students and other young people, who clearly did not understand the phrase "Sunday best," were as shabbily dressed as ever. Patience, however, was dressed properly and greeted Elizabeth warmly. The two women stood to one side of the Meetinghouse door and tried to catch up on their news.

"Things are settled at Harvard for Janet Stevens," began Elizabeth, "and I'll tell you about what happened there sometime soon."

"I'm so glad if her troubles are over," said Patience. "Is the police situation cleared up, too?"

"Yes," answered Elizabeth. "There were several unfortunate things going on in that department. Evil things, really, starting with plagiarism and cheating and ending up with blackmail and murder." Elizabeth decided this was not the time to speak of her internal distress about some of the things she had done. She rationalized that there was not time to tell Patience everything before Meeting began.

"Oh, dear!" said Patience. "I'm not sure I want thee to tell me the details. But I'm happy for Janet and for thee." She looked at a clump of Quakers entering the Meetinghouse. "Thee may be a little out of touch with the news here. Hugo Coleman is now saying that perhaps the handicap ramp could run from the front door to the sidewalk."

The Clerk could not help but smile. "That's quite a change," she said, "and it seems a change for the better."

"It's the only convenient place for it to be, in the opinion of us ancients," said Patience. "And we're the ones who would use it. Once it's been there for a while, I hope it won't look so much like a scar on the old building as some Friends were thinking."

"I wonder what changed his mind," said Elizabeth.

"Well, thee asked us to pray about it. Don't be surprised if prayer has results!"

Elizabeth Elliot smiled at her old friend.

"And now it's time to go in for worship," said Patience firmly. With the help of her cane she maneuvered up the stairs and through the door.

The Clerk sat down on her favorite bench and looked around at the familiar faces in the big room. She wondered if Quakers were not better off without Easter celebrations. Those denominations which observed Easter in special ways found they saw some members of their congregations only on that Sunday. In any event, Elizabeth thought hopefully, however we worship, we should be able to agree with our church cousins that the Resurrection is real to us, on this day and all days.

Turning her mind to prayer, the Clerk repeated the opening section of the fourth Gospel to herself.

" 'In the beginning was the Word, and the Word was God . . .' " Soon the Clerk was lost to what was happening in the room. But the beginning of John's Gospel was not as illuminating to her as usual. She stumbled on the passages about the Light and then had tremendous difficulty focusing on the Scripture at all. Confused, the Clerk began to realize how deep was her internal conflict.

When Elizabeth returned to an awareness of the

Meetinghouse, she found that even the tardiest of Friends had taken their places. She felt drained. Looking at her watch, the Clerk found that worship was about half over.

The pain that had been growing within her for the past week broke through her internal barriers. The Clerk felt grief and guilt washing over her. Quaker silence had brought her back to herself. Her arrogance had led her to overestimate what she could do for Andrew's childhood friend. She had not heeded Ralph's warnings about what life had been like for John Anderson. Her compassion had been of God, but her actions had not. Elizabeth Elliot repented of her actions. She prayed for forgiveness and for the wisdom not to repeat her mistake.

She felt some relief from her guilt. But she struggled against the voice of the silence around her. Could everything she had done concerning Janet have been wrong too? Her stubborn indignation mounted up in her mind. She felt a surge of self-righteousness and knew, even while she was most firmly in its grip, she must have been in the wrong.

But what was I supposed to do? she thought desperately to herself. That girl was in agony. She'd been mistreated by that man. And by the men who turned their faces away from her.

The Clerk sighed. The silence around her seemed oppressive, and she shifted her weight on the bench in her agitation to escape from it. But for a lifelong Quaker, there was no escape.

The lies I told and the looking around I did, she

thought to herself, I suppose I must admit they were wrong. Perhaps I let Ruth's cynicism infect me. But the need was great, and I accomplished a lot of good!

The silence gave her no comfort. She began, very quietly, to cry. A few minutes passed and the Clerk was able to contain her emotions. She hoped she had not unduly disturbed the worshippers around her, but since Quaker silence often led to strong feelings she did not feel apologetic about tears.

Joel Timmermann, in a corner of the Meeting-house, rose to speak. He looked around at the assembled Quakers. The Clerk immediately felt her indignation against him well up. For the present, her own self-judgment was suspended.

Joel's voice broke harshly through the silence. "Friends, I've been quite wrong about something at the university where I work. There have been problems there, serious problems, that I've been ignoring.

"It wasn't easy to admit to myself how narrow and selfish I've been. I'd never really thought about what professional work in an all-male department might be like for a woman. As a matter of my own convenience, I'd been too quick to dismiss any problems that women in university life experienced. I thought they were exaggerating. Perhaps I even thought their troubles were their own fault.

"Today I feel called to say that if there's hope for a bigoted old man like me, I think this Meeting can take a lot of credit for it."

Something akin to shame filled Elizabeth. Tears again filled her eyes. It was disorienting that Joel Tim-

mermann could admit what he was and how wrong
he had been. Immediately, self-righteousness resur-
faced in the Clerk and she thought: He doesn't know
more grace than me!

Then, as quickly as the shame had entered her,
Elizabeth felt something deeper and stronger. She
looked back at her struggle with herself over the past
two weeks. She had known what she was doing would
not hold up to the inspection of a Quaker conscience.
She had known that but suppressed her understanding
so she could help Janet Stevens. The things she had
done were not crimes. But she regretted them. The
deceit did not sit well with her. It was not part of the
Light that could enter into this world, and her actions
therefore could not be seen as a Christian witness, at
least not by Quaker standards. She could forgive herself, because her actions had been motivated by compassion. Her anger with Joel, she realized, was also
acceptable in Meeting life. But, admitted the Clerk to
herself, he has acknowledged his error. Elizabeth
knew she must do the same. Relaxing into the calm
that this thought produced, she quickly found her way
into a deep state of prayer.

No one else spoke and when Elizabeth next looked
at her watch she realized that more than an hour of
worship had passed. She felt it right to end the Meeting by shaking hands with her neighbor. All around
the room Quakers shook hands with those nearest
them and quietly said, "Good Morning, Friend." Jane
Thompson rose and made a long announcement about
the need for more volunteers in the used-clothing

room in the basement. A major shipment of clothes to the Friends' Service Committee in Philadelphia was being organized, and the women who worked in the clothing room needed help in boxing up what the wealthy people of Cambridge had donated. After the announcement, the Meeting broke.

The crowds were thick as Elizabeth tried to make her way to the bus stop at Harvard Square. The transfer point for bus riders had been located underground by the city authorities who thought that, since the subway station was underground, those who wanted to catch a bus might enjoy wading through a sea of humans to the middle of the Square and descending into the darkness of the earth with the crowd of train riders. The buses emerged from their underground tunnels several blocks north and south of the Square and did not stop for several blocks beyond that. The crowded condition of the Square today, both above and below ground, was worse than Elizabeth could remember. Catholics, Protestants, and vague Christians turned out for divine services on Easter. Harvard Square gave people an abundance of denominational choices, and Harvard lent the churches a certain cachet. Not even the mass on Christmas Eve attracted so many of the shallowly committed. Elizabeth caught the Watertown bus that went upriver along Mt. Auburn Street, and was glad when it emerged again into the daylight. She got off at the bus stop nearest Mt. Auburn cemetery.

She had not wanted to drive through the Easter traffic and was glad that there was another option besides walking. She felt calmer than she had in the middle of Meeting, but she was still deep in thought. She walked into the cemetery and turned her steps toward the northern boundary of the grounds, where her husband's grave lay. Several juncos and a jay flew near the Clerk, but she did not see them, intent as she was on her goal.

Michael's grave with its marble headstone looked just as it always had. Elizabeth read the text on the stone and remembered the day that Friends Meeting had held a memorial in honor of her husband's life. His body had not been present. Before the memorial meeting, the undertaker had interred the body without Elizabeth and her children feeling the need to be witnesses. But, off and on in the years that had followed, Elizabeth made visits to the grave. There was a plot reserved for her, and her name was already inscribed on the large marble stone which she had chosen. Once or twice, when she was in Neil Stevenson's company, she had wondered about the prospects of their marrying. The tombstone had made no allowance for that. The Clerk felt no regrets about the stone she had ordered. She had spent her life with Michael, not with Neil, and memories of her children when they were young were wound together with memories of her husband.

In the early years of her widowhood, Elizabeth had felt separated from her husband. But on this Easter visit she recognized how thin the barrier between them was. Although the Clerk's life had no room for a formal observance of the Resurrection, the idea was woven into all her thoughts. And the triumph of life was linked to her certainty that she and her husband were not far apart. She remembered the disciples, shortly after the Crucifixion, on the road to Emmaus. They had met a stranger to whom they explained that the women of their party had seen angels proclaiming that Jesus was alive. The immediacy of the Resurrection swept through the Quaker. She repeated softly to herself the words of Paul: "For as in Adam all die, even so in Christ shall all be made alive."

Elizabeth believed deeply in the words and found evidence for them all around her. In her simple faith, even men like Paul Chadwick were part of God's creation and would, in the end, be led back home. She paused in her thoughts for an instant to pray for the peace of the dead scientist.

Looking at her watch, Elizabeth decided she needed to start home for a late lunch. She was not satisfied that her soul had yet accomplished what it needed, but she left the cemetery and stood on the street, waiting for a bus. She could catch a glimpse of the cherry trees on the river from where she stood, but they were not yet in bloom. The bus came and took her away from thoughts of her husband. She rode back to the Square on the sunny side of the bus until it descended into the earth. As Elizabeth climbed up the stairs from the underground bus stop at Harvard Square, she was glad to see the crowds had thinned. To her surprise, at the top of the stairs, Detective

Burnham was just appearing. Catching sight of her, he stood on the sidewalk and waited for her to come the last few steps up into the daylight.

"Good afternoon, Mrs. Elliot," said the detective. "I guess you meet everyone in the Square on a day like this."

"Yes," said Elizabeth. "This morning the crowds were the thickest I've ever seen."

"I failed to thank you when I left the secretary's office on Friday. Rather rude of me, of course, but I was worried Kolakowski would be on the run, so I wanted to hurry."

Elizabeth smiled. "His whole life had been focused on his work, and he valued his career so highly he was willing to cheat and to kill for it. So I didn't think he'd go far."

"You were right. I arrested him on the murder charge. I took him down to Central Square, where the transcriber could barely keep up with his confession. As for Forrest Lang, Eric will bring a charge of blackmail against him. Eric says he's leaving science to go into his father's business—some sort of merchandising in New York. Anyway, he no longer cares about his professional credentials being questioned because of plagiarism, so he's willing to testify against his blackmailer. We picked Forrest up on Saturday. He's not talking, but we don't need his evidence. Eric's testimony will be enough."

"I'm glad the truth has come out," said the Quaker, "and I hope in the long run it will be for the best, even for Professor Kolakowski and Forrest Lang."

"Maybe not, but it's in the interest of justice! And that's what matters in the end. Anyway, even though I don't follow how you put the whole story together, I'm glad to thank you for your help."

Elizabeth inclined her head toward Burnham in response. He said good-bye and disappeared down the stairs.

Fresh news of Peter Kolakowski and Forrest Lang was enough to make any Quaker long for prayer. As she rounded the corner into Garden Street she saw that the doors to Christ Church, facing Cambridge Common, were standing open. Some Quakers would never venture into a church, but Elizabeth was sure that God could be found anywhere, and she wanted to sit down someplace quiet. She entered the stately Episcopal church, walking past carefully preserved bullet holes from the Revolutionary War.

It was now mid-afternoon, and the historic sanctuary was empty. On both sides the windows were halfway open, letting in the spring air. In the morning the building had been packed with worshippers, but the wooden structure was calm and quiet now, just as a Quaker might wish. Many pots of lilies lined the altar and stood on the wide windowsills, echoing the white altar cloth and the white banner hung from the high, cantilevered pulpit.

Elizabeth Elliot had always loved lilies. Because her parents had been strict Quakers, and lilies were used as decoration in churches, the flowers had never been in their house. But Elizabeth had been introduced to them in the homes of neighbors. They still reminded her of childhood joy.

The Clerk sat down near a window hoping to smell the lilies above her on the window ledge. She quickly and gladly settled down for prayer, drawing her mind away from Michael, from murder, from Joel Timmermann, from newly released prisoners, and from Janet. In the peace of prayer, from the center of her mind, Elizabeth felt ideas and words flowing upwards. She waited patiently for them to reach the surface. So much had happened since the biting cold of February. She had done a great deal and regretted most of it. But today she had acknowledged and confessed to herself what her transgression had been. She resolved to try, once more, to set aside her own will in favor of something else. As she sat stiffly in the pew, the image of Mary at the Annunciation broke into her mind.

" ' . . . let it be to me according to thy word,' " the Clerk murmurs from the Scriptures. The lilies on the windowsill sway gently in the breeze as if in answer.

QUAKER SILENCE

AN ELIZABETH ELLIOT MYSTERY

IRENE ALLEN

When Elizabeth Elliot receives the shocking news that a prominent member of the Quaker Meeting she belongs to has been found murdered in his garden, she must sift through a myriad of red herrings and seemingly unrelated clues and secrets to uncover a killer amongst her own. For within the blessed "Quaker silence" is greed, forbidden love, and vengeful anger struggling to find a voice.

"Like her heroine, [Irene Allen] speaks softly . . . but like the Quaker practice of silent prayer, her storytelling methods have their own quiet power." —*The New York Times Book Review*

"A wonderful first novel . . . [that is] exquisitely written in a confident, smoothly paced, yet almost reverent, tone."
—*San Francisco Examiner-Chronicle*

COMING SOON FROM
ST. MARTIN'S PAPERBACKS